IN DEAD MAN'S ALLEY

W❃RLDWIDE.

TORONTO • NEW YORK • LONDON
AMSTERDAM • PARIS • SYDNEY • HAMBURG
STOCKHOLM • ATHENS • TOKYO • MILAN
MADRID • WARSAW • BUDAPEST • AUCKLAND

IN DEAD MAN'S ALLEY

A Worldwide Mystery/May 2009

First published by Hilliard & Harris.

ISBN-13: 978-0-373-26673-9
ISBN-10:   0-373-26673-1

Printed in U.S.A.

For my family

ONE

DEEDRA MASEFIELD was seated at her desk in the newsroom of the *Daily Spokesman* early that Monday morning when Clete Bailey, the editor, buzzed her from his office. As she hurried through the newsroom, she wondered what she had done now to earn Clete's ire. Nervously she ran a hand through her short blond curls, curls that framed a piquant face. It was an impish face that could smile with mirth and gladness, or grow taut with anger, her sea-blue eyes flashing sparks.

"Know a guy named Matt Brandon?" Clete barked before she was even seated.

"Yep. Remember the Curtis murder case?"

"Oh, yeah. Well, he's on the phone, says he has some info for you." Clete gestured to his phone.

Deedra experienced surprise, her hand unsteady. "Hello, Matt."

"Hi, Deedra. Guess you didn't expect to hear from me?"

Then ensued a discussion of mutual acquaintances during which time Deedra impatiently waited to learn the importance and purpose of Matt Brandon's call. He was a busy sheriff and normally wouldn't waste time on a social call, wouldn't need to call her unless it was important.

"Have you heard of the discovery of those prehistoric mixosaurus bones over at a ghost town called North Ledge?"

"Yes, a news break last week."

"Actually, the discovery of those old bones was made months ago. Deedra, they've had a murder up there and Sheriff Gavin Blair asked me about you. He sort of requested your presence up there to help him out. They don't want a lot of media people there; the scientists claim it would spoil the dig. The place is filled with them, and they sure are particular about who gets in to see their work. There are also several artists and writers living in the old hotel. An interesting and eccentric group, I understand. Anyway, Gavin thought a news investigator like you could represent the media and still help out in the investigation: perhaps learn things from those people he hasn't been able to. He indicated that he would like to keep a friend of yours from being convicted of murder."

Deedra ignored the word "friend." Lots of people claimed to be her friend, when a lot of times she had no idea who they were. It sometimes happened to people who earned reputations as news investigators.

"Who was murdered?"

There was a pause as if Matt wondered why she didn't ask the friend's name. "A woman named Rhonda Adams. The main suspect is a young geologist named Gregg Dancer. Know him?"

"Gregg Dancer!" Deedra felt her heart skip a beat, then plunge on in frantic fluttering. She suddenly experienced difficulty in breathing. Gregg Dancer was an old flame from her childhood. His parents had lived next door to hers in the small California town she still called home. They had drifted apart when Gregg had attended a different college to pursue a career in geology. Deedra had heard that he was quite successful, sometimes acting as a consultant for large mining companies. Now that vibrant young man was in trouble, deep trouble. Deedra suddenly remembered in a flash his teenaged smile.

"Why is he suspected of murdering this Rhonda Adams?"

"His knife was used as the murder weapon and they had argued the evening before. A really loud argument. She was knifed in the back. Her murderer snuck up on her in an alley appropriately named Dead Man's Alley. You have to realize this is a ghost town, hasn't been restored like some of the others in the old California gold country. Like North San Juan, for instance. Gregg Dancer is living in the old Wells Fargo building in North Ledge. Gavin hasn't arrested him yet and doesn't believe he's the killer. But the D.A. is seeking a quick arrest and conviction. He's running for reelection."

Deedra sighed. "I'll have to get Clete Bailey to assign me to this. I certainly want to try and help Gregg."

"Will this complicate things between you and Deke Thomas?"

"Deke doesn't have reins on me, Matt, and he hasn't been able to make up his mind whether to marry me or not. I'm a free woman now…looking for someone else. I could end up an old maid waiting around for Deke to make up his mind."

Matt laughed. "Might not hurt to give him some competition."

"Right."

"There's another friend of yours up here. I think Gavin suspects him even more than he suspects Gregg. Another geologist named Frank Shundo."

Deedra's thoughts few back to the quiet boy who sat across the aisle from her in U.S. History class in high school, the seat right behind Gregg Dancer. Surely Frank could not be suspected of knifing someone in the back! If he killed anyone, he would want to look them right in the eyes.

"Deedra, can I tell Gavin you're on your way up to North Ledge? He'll be waiting for you in an empty saloon across the alley from the old Wells Fargo station."

"Tell him I'm on my way," Deedra felt an unusual excitement as she turned to Clete. "I'd like to be assigned to this murder case in that old ghost town where they discovered those old fossil bones. Remember the story we ran last week? A mixosaur find at a place called North Ledge. A guy named Gregg Dancer is suspected of murdering a woman named Rhonda Adams. My family used to investigate old ghost towns and mines in that part of California so I know it very well. Sometimes those trips when I was young included Gregg Dancer and his family so I'd have a great way of getting the real story. Gregg went into geology, and I settled for this news reporting life. We sort of had a crush on each other in those days. Gregg's the main suspect. The sheriff there doubts that he's guilty, but they've got an over-zealous D.A. who is up for reelection."

Clete noted her excitement, how her blue eyes flashed with anticipation, and nodded, "What will I tell Deke Thomas when he gets back to the U.S.?"

"Just that I'm out of town on a murder story."

"No mention of this Gregg Dancer?"

Deedra looked Clete squarely in the eyes. "I don't care what you tell Deke. He isn't my keeper, you know. And he obviously isn't in favor of marriage. Why is everyone so interested anyway?"

WHILE DEEDRA WAS SHOPPING for outdoor gear, she arranged to have her 4-wheel rig serviced, and was suddenly glad she was eccentric enough to own one. Bad weather wouldn't slow her down. She was anxious to see her old friend again and wondered how he was getting along after his ego-bruising divorce from Mary Jane, who was now married to Alfred Shepley, another geologist.

She purchased a shovel, rope, food that could be easily prepared or eaten cold, lanterns, flashlights, candles, and matches. She was familiar with the lack of electricity and running water in old ghost towns.

NORTH LEDGE WAS LOCATED in Nevada County. Deedra left the highway at Marysville, driving through the old gold towns of Rough-and-Ready, Grass Valley, and Nevada City. They had long since ceased to be ghost towns. Residents had repaired old buildings and added new ones. The towns were very much alive and the busy streets of Nevada City inviting. She would have liked to have had time to browse there since it had kept much of its 1800s influence but she was in a hurry to reach her destination.

Turning north toward North San Juan, she found the road steep and narrow, though paved and meandering through forest and meadow. Swimmers had gathered along the banks of the South Fork of the Yuba River which looked clean and inviting from the road above. Several hundred people still lived in North San Juan along with the remnants of brick buildings, a post office, a store, and a gas station. Mine tailings dotted the hillsides showing scars of hydraulic mining when they had used the water from the Yuba River. Just beyond the town she turned east on a very rutty, dusty road that showed signs of recent travel despite its decrepit condition.

North Ledge was not one of the popular tourist gold towns. It was indeed still a ghost town. Deedra had never heard of it before the news of the mixosaur find and was eager to see the place, glad to get out of the city which sweltered under the hot July sun. The air was fresh, and though it was late afternoon, there was a stirring breeze that swept across the dusty road. Here and there where time had destroyed the road, Deedra was forced to drive around boulders and scraggly trees. She couldn't take her eyes off the treacherous road long enough to study the country. Though the way to North Ledge was not long in miles, it took several hours to traverse, and it was dusk when she finally drove over a rickety bridge and stopped in front of the Wells Fargo building.

It was a larger town than she had expected. Trees lined Jackson Creek, soft lantern light streaked through new screens that had been nailed across the broken windows. The light indicated that Gregg was home.

From the saloon next door, a tall rugged man in a sheriff's uniform with a thatch of close-cropped hair, stern features, and jutting ears, stepped into the thick dust of the street.

"I'm Deedra Masefield," she informed the lawman.

The stern features parted in one of the most infectious grins Deedra had ever seen. "I'm Gavin Blair. Matt said you were on your way. I was beginning to worry. This part of the country doesn't feature the best of roads."

Deedra laughed and gestured toward her 4-wheel rig. "That can go anywhere."

"Come on in and I'll tell you what's been going on. Then I'll take you over to see Gregg. I'm having you bunk in the old Catholic Church. I cleaned it up today and put a latch on the door."

Deedra nodded acquiescence as she walked into the archaic saloon that had been turned into a sheriff's office. There was a cot in one corner. The makeshift desk was a wooden plank laid across saw horses. Gavin Blair gestured her to a nail barrel turned upside down. "Best seat I can offer." Then he filled her in on the Rhonda Adams murder.

"First of all, I'll tell you how I knew you were a friend of Gregg's. When we searched his things we found a newspaper picture and story about you in his wallet. Matt Brandon filled me in on your help with the Curtis murder case." The sheriff gulped coffee with a rather loud slurp. "Rhonda Adams was killed day before yesterday. I'm waiting on the autopsy report to find out exactly when. I suspect it was right after dark, between 9:30 and 10:00. There's just no positive proof where everyone was at that time. Don't even know where Rhonda had been." He pointed to the alley that ran between the Wells Fargo office and an empty store with old fashioned gingerbread working on the store front. "Gregg found her in the morning. He says he was up early and going to the old swimming hole to wash up.

I'm surprised that no one found her the night before. But it gets so damn dark up here if there's no moonlight. Someone could have walked right by her and might not have seen her there if they didn't have a flashlight."

"Tell me about the people up here."

Gavin Blair leaned his straight-backed chair against the rough planked wall. "That's the difficulty. There are almost too many suspects. Matt probably told you that Frank Shundo is here, lives in that old store across the street." Gavin jerked his thumb to a building cloaked in heavy shadow. "He's been in this area for several weeks examining old mines for the Sierra Mining Company. He's their head mining engineer, and was the one who told Gregg Dancer about the mixosaurus find."

"Then why is Gregg the main suspect?"

"The knife that killed Rhonda Adams has his initials scratched into the handle, though Gregg claims the knife isn't his. Rhonda was facedown in the dirt. She was probably heading toward the old swimming hole for a bath. It's next to the livery stable. Both the blacksmith shop and livery stable are vacant. The odd thing is that Rhonda couldn't swim and seldom went to the swimming hole to bathe. She usually went further up the creek."

"They use the creek to bathe in then?"

"Yeah. There's also a well out back of the old Frontier Hotel where we get our drinking water. But it's a shallow well and would go dry without careful economy."

"Were Gregg's fingerprints on the knife?"

"No. No fingerprints at all."

Deedra saw a shadow move against the wall, a scary flickering movement. She looked toward the doorway where Frank Shundo stood, his eyes glittering in the lantern light. He was staring at Deedra as if she was a ghost, his face pale and tense. Was it fright Deedra saw in his eyes?

TWO

"HELLO, DEEDRA! Why are you up here?" Frank Shundo's voice squeaked, reflecting the look of strain on his face.

"I'm here about a story on that mixosaurus discovery, Frank. Right now I'm being filled in on Rhonda Adams's murder."

She saw Frank Shundo relax. Suddenly the fear that Frank was the killer caused her to give Gavin Blair a speculative look.

Frank knew she was an investigative reporter, but also knew of her rock-hound hobby, her penchant for investigating old ghost towns. Why had the fact that she was in North Ledge upset him? Did he think his mining engineer position was threatened by adverse publicity? Or worried that Deedra might unravel the truth about the murder?

"I'll talk to you tomorrow, Deedra. I just wanted to find out who was up here since Sheriff Blair has placed North Ledge off limits." Without waiting for a reply, Frank disappeared into the night.

In a few minutes they heard the squeak of the door across the street.

"Why didn't we hear him open that door?" Deedra asked.

"He wasn't in there. I saw him up the street by that old hotel talking to Derryck Evans a few minutes ago."

"Derryck Evans?"

"He's one of the group of artists and writers living in the old Frontier Hotel. There are six of them counting Rhonda. They've each taken several rooms and converted them into studios and living quarters. They've been up here since early spring. Seems they want to devote all their time to their art and this is a cheap place to live. An interesting group. None of them liked Rhonda Adams. She was tough and quite capable of taking care of herself except that she got herself killed. A mixosaurus bone was found next to her as if she had dropped it when she was stabbed."

Deedra frowned. "Do you think that implicates one of the scientists?"

"Can't say. Gregg said the bone wasn't one they had found at the dig and the scientists are mum about it. I suspect there's something of a mystery about that bone, and who had it, and what significance it had to Rhonda…or to the killer."

Gavin paused a moment before continuing. "They tell me Rhonda was in love with Gregg. The situation's complicated by the fact that Mary Jane Shepley, Gregg's ex-wife, is here with her present husband, Alfred Shepley. They're living in that old saloon at the far end of the street across from the hotel. Now as I understand it, there is a rumor Gregg is actually in love with Valerie Penrose. She's one of the artists up at the old hotel. I have a hunch Mary Jane is upset about Gregg's being in love with someone else even though they're divorced."

Deedra felt her heart skip a beat. A twinge of hurt flooded through her. She had rather hoped that she and Gregg could renew their teenage romance. She sighed. Why did she always fall for men who didn't care for her? Then a stab of guilt struck her. Deke did love her—

she knew that. He just didn't want the encumbrance of marriage. And she did. She wanted a secure home and children, but supposed she would end up a career woman without a family.

"Mary Jane?" she asked absently. "What the heck is she doing up in Gregg's vicinity? I had heard their divorce was bitter and humiliating for Gregg."

"Shepley's a paleontologist at the university where Gregg lectures. Shepley is jealous because Gregg identified the mixosaurus bones first even before Shepley knew they existed. He says he's the paleontologist, not Gregg. As far as I can determine, Shepley is jealous of Gregg because of his work and status more than because he was married to Mary Jane first. It's a strong motive to kill Gregg, but not Rhonda. And I think Mary Jane is still in love with Gregg, and he won't have anything to do with her."

"You did know Mary Jane was a neighbor of mine for a year or so when we were all youngsters in that small town? She chased Gregg even then," Deedra ventured.

"Do you think she has the capability to kill? She knew that Rhonda was in love with Gregg, and may have wanted to eliminate the competition."

"Yes, I'm certain she's capable, but she isn't stupid. I doubt she would kill without a very, very strong motive. I saw her torment a crippled cat once. She has a cruel streak."

Sheriff Blair raised an eyebrow, and sighed while he made notations in his black notebook.

"All the scientists except Alfred Shepley live in that large brick building just behind Frank Shundo's place. The one facing Bridge Street. They're all professors at different colleges, experts in geology, anthropology, and paleontology, and they just won't give me the time of day. They spend most of their time in the dig even taking their lunches with them. When I go up there, they clam up. I actually had to get a warrant to look at those old fossils. Old Dr. Von Kraus stood there with a rifle in his hands as if he thought I was going to steal the damn things."

Deedra grinned in sympathy. "Then the suspects are Gregg, Frank, the five artists, the three scientists, and Alfred and Mary Jane Shepley?"

"Yes. Twelve in all. And unless I can prove someone else is the killer, Gregg Dancer will probably be charged with Rhonda's murder."

"You don't think he did it?"

"No. He isn't the type to stab anyone in the back, and just because Rhonda was in love with him isn't motive enough to convince me. But there's the evidence of the knife."

Deedra nodded. "But someone could be framing him. Let's go see Gregg."

GREGG ANSWERED Gavin's knock with a frown of annoyance that quickly disappeared at the surprise of seeing Deedra. "Deedra! What the hell are you doing in these remote mountains?" He grabbed her in a tight squeeze.

"Never mind that, let me in and tell me what's been going on. And I want a story about that old mixosaurus."

Deedra glanced around. Gregg had created a work room with long counters holding a spectograph for identification of minerals, solutions for testing purposes, a polarizing microscope, copies of books on minerals, among them John Sinkanka's *Gemstones and Minerals*.

There were several samples in which Deedra saw traces of azurite, just a thin coating of it over porphyry rock.

"Copper around here?" Deedra was aware that azurite was a copper mineral.

"Not that I can find, though Frank Shundo keeps searching."

Deedra didn't ask where he had obtained the azurite samples. Gregg evidently had a reason for not volunteering the information. Where there were samples of such minerals indicated that more valuable minerals, gems even, might also be found. As a rock-hound, a searcher of interesting rocks and fossils, she could appreciate his secrecy.

"Don't you have a set of Dana?" she asked. Noting Gavin's puzzled look, she explained. "Practically every geologist's bible, a set of four books titled *Dana's System of Mineralogy*."

"They're in the back of my rig," Gregg replied. "Here's a stratum drawing of the mixosaur site." He handed her a neat drawing.

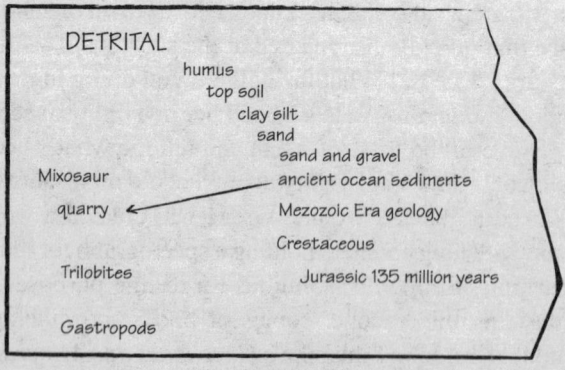

DETRITAL

humus
    top soil
        clay silt
            sand
                sand and gravel
Mixosaur   ancient ocean sediments
    quarry ←   Mezozoic Era geology
                        Crestaceous
Trilobites   Jurassic 135 million years

Gastropods

On another page, which he didn't mean for her to see was another drawing, a most interesting one. It looked to Deedra's amateur eyes much like a sketch of gemstones "in situ."

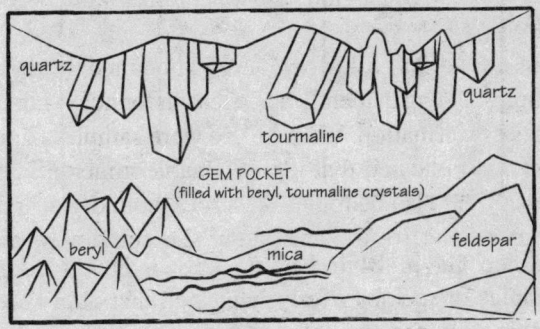

quartz

quartz

tourmaline

GEM POCKET
(filled with beryl, tourmaline crystals)

beryl

mica

feldspar

HIMALAYA

The word "Himalaya" printed under the sketch was somehow familiar. She had seen a drawing similar to that somewhere. She was aware that Gregg was watching her closely, perhaps hoping she wouldn't recognize the sketch, and quite aware of her amateur gemological status.

She glanced at Gavin, and he made an excuse about getting a lantern so he could show Deedra to her lodging in the old church.

When they heard Gavin open the door to his saloon office, Deedra asked, "Did you kill her, Gregg?"

"No, Deedra, I didn't. I just don't know how to prove I didn't." Gregg sounded forlorn, desolate.

By the time Gavin Blair returned, they were talking of old times and old friends.

On the workbench Deedra saw a sketch Gregg had evidently just completed. She noted the copper formulas with increasing curiosity.

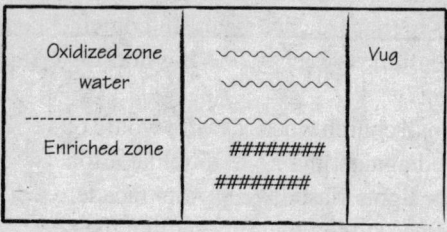

Since Gavin Blair had no knowledge of copper formulas or seemed overly interested that didn't seem anything mysterious about the drawing. Gregg was a geologist after all and probably had many drawings no one else could understand.

"Do you keep a daily record of the dig?" she asked.

He nodded and showed her a well-worn leather notebook containing his neat handwriting.

"This dig is important?" Deedra wished she could read the daily entries he'd made.

"Yes, very. We've uncovered some rare finds, things I'm not at liberty to tell you about."

Gavin Blair interrupted. "We'll talk later. I'll take you over to the church and you can get settled. Did you bring a sleeping bag?"

Deedra nodded. "Yes. I didn't expect to find modern conveniences."

They took their leave. Gavin Blair grinned as he climbed into the 4-wheel rig. "Glad you came prepared," he said.

THEY DROVE OVER the bridge spanning Jackson Creek and up the old stage road leading north. The church was located on a knoll about half a block from Gavin's office. It had been abandoned since World War II when the mines in that area had been shut down. The inhabitants had all moved away leaving nothing but ghostly memories.

The small church where Deedra would be staying was silhouetted against the night sky like a lonely sentinel. As the car lights flashed across its facade, Deedra saw the cross was still on the roof, though the bell had been removed from the bell tower. Wooden steps led up to the Gothic-type door, and a lean-to was attached to the north side where she surmised that the priest had lived.

Gavin lit the lantern and they stumbled up the wooden steps. The door screeched gently as Gavin pushed it open. There was not a stick of furniture there, not a pew left.

"Did souvenir hunters strip this church?"

"No. Everything was moved over to another city on the Yuba River." Gavin glanced at her. "Scared? It's rather isolated here."

"No. I don't think the killer would be after me…yet." She laughed and was surprised to find that the sound of it echoed mockingly around the old church.

It didn't amuse Gavin and Deedra saw him frown. He hesitated as if reluctant to leave her there. He was still frowning when he strode back toward his makeshift office, the beam of his flashlight like the gleam of a firefly in the darkness.

Deedra shivered, glad she didn't have to sleep in the open. She had an unnatural fear of snakes…and rats.

BIRDS WERE CHIRPING in the trees along Jackson Creek when she woke up the next morning. She was tired and achy from her uncomfortable night in the sleeping bag. It was easy for a person, she mused, to get too used to soft beds and comfortable living.

Someone was walking on the road toward North Ledge. She peered through the broken slats in the wall to see who was such an early riser. A tall young man with broad shoulders and a mop of unruly hair, a camera slung over his shoulder, stopped beside a 4-wheel rig like Deedra's, only it had a news insignia on the door.

Deedra recognized Brent Larsen of the News-Transcriber with immediate excitement. Brent was a colleague she had often competed with, and sometimes worked with, on various news stories. She had a secret admiration for Brent, admired his news know-how. Though like Deke, he was not the marrying kind. She sighed. Why did she always meet and become attracted to men with that kind of personality? Lately, she and Brent had been working on the same news stories and their paths had often crossed. Brent had a background in law enforcement and he made an excellent investigative reporter. When they did work together, he specialized in getting the photos, and usually Deedra got the front page bylines. Though Deedra had to admit there were times when Brent had beat her to the scoop. She often wondered if that was part of her admiration for him, infatuation for Brent because they were in constant competition. Would she admire him like that if he was in some other profession?

Deedra dressed rapidly. She was already missing her normal morning bath, and not really liking her cold breakfast. She had to find out what Brent was doing up here. She didn't want him to know that she was assisting the sheriff.

When she hurried down the church steps, Brent had disappeared, though his 4-wheel rig was still parked in front of Gavin's quarters. A movement along Jackson Creek near the old blacksmith's shop caught her attention. Brent was walking along the creek.

When she crossed the bridge she saw him with his ever-present camera slung over his shoulder. Just the sight of him caused her a tinge of excitement. He was dressed in jeans and T-shirt, and heavy hiking boots. He walked with his head down as if searching the creek bed.

Deedra raced up the creek, intercepting Brent at a place where they old livery stable shielded them from being seen by anyone at the old hotel, or Gregg in his quarters.

"Brent, what are you doing here?"

"Hi! I heard you were seen driving out of town after buying outdoor equipment. I reckoned I would find you up here. I tried to pump Clete, but he only said you were out of town on a story. Actually, I bribed Ben Anderson. He had overheard Clete tell someone where you were."

"I'm here at the request of Sheriff Blair, though I'm just supposed to be covering the mixosaur find."

Brent's gray-blue eyes suddenly glinted with interest. "What's happened up here?"

"Murder. A woman named Rhonda Adams. An old friend of mine is suspected of stabbing her in the back. And the sheriff can't get any information from the scientists on the dig. He thinks the murder might be connected with the fossil find since a mixosaur bone was found beside the body."

Brent murmured something and ran one of his well-manicured hands through his tangle of hair.

Deedra looked away. She must never let Brent see how much she cared for him, knew that she must always keep everything on a mutual work basis. She didn't want to get hurt again, not the type of hurt that Deke had caused her. But Brent was very like Deke in many ways, and wasn't about to get "trapped into marriage." Brent had been married twice, and was woman-shy now. Anyway, Deedra didn't think she could break down his reserve. She was a good reporter, not a beautiful femme fatale. Men liked to talk to her, admired her investigative skills, but they didn't glamorize her. She sighed.

"Where is this mixosaur find?" Brent glanced toward the mountains.

"I'm not sure. I think it's up on Feather Mountain. Out that old stage road," Deedra pointed past the church. There was a line of broken down shanties, many only a pile of weathered-out lumber. Beyond was a jagged mountain still in partial shadow. It looked somber and mysterious in the early morning light.

"Who are the suspects right now?"

"Gregg Dancer and another school friend of mine, Frank Shundo. The murder weapon has Gregg's initials on it."

"Wow!"

"I can't envision either Gregg or Frank as the murderer, Brent. Frank was always such a quiet, well-mannered boy. He's third generation American, though knives are traditional Japanese weapons, I suppose. I'd hate to think either Gregg or Frank ended up as killers." Again she recalled their youthful laughter.

"There's Gavin Blair now," Deedra pointed to the

rugged man striding across the old bridge going toward the church. "Gavin! Over here!"

The sheriff turned, waved, and began a long striding toward them. Deedra noted that he quickly assessed Brent Larsen, wondering why he was here, though the camera probably gave him a good idea.

"Gavin, this is Brent Larsen of the News-Transcriber. Is it all right if he stays? I know you've put North Ledge off limits."

Gavin studied Brent, determining whether Brent could be trusted. "Yes. I may need his help. And I do need copies of photos. The D.A. takes everything, and I'm often left having to request photos. I'll permit you to stay, Brent Larsen, on one condition. I don't want any more reporters up here. You'll make certain you don't attract any, agreed?"

"Agreed."

"Anything happen overnight, Gavin?" Deedra inquired.

"No. I haven't seen anyone this morning. The scientists usually head up Feather Mountain early, but they haven't left yet this morning. That probably means they're running tests. They have a crude lab in that big old store building." Gavin pointed to a large brick building with evidences of recent repair. It fronted on Bridge Street.

The main street was named Frontier Street. Dead Man's Alley ran between the Wells Fargo Office and an unoccupied store building. At the far end of Dead Man's Alley were the old livery stables and the blacksmith shop, both on the banks of Jackson Creek.

There was movement around the old Frontier Hotel indicating that some of the young people were up and about.

Deedra was eager to meet them, felt a stirring of excitement about it. Who was into their art so much that they would choose to live in an abandoned hotel in a ghost town? The very atmosphere sent her nerves tingling, her writer's imagination soaring. It was an appropriate setting for a murder, all right. The thought that those young artists had a whole summer with nothing more to do than write or paint was a heady thought.

"Guess you'd better bunk in that old store next to Dead Man's Alley, Brent. There just isn't a whole hell of a lot of accommodations around here. But that old building is in fair shape. It won't fall down on you, anyway."

The store building was decorated in hand-carved "gingerbread" workings, a more sturdy looking structure than the saloon next to the store where Frank Shundo bunked. It was the only vacant building since Alfred and Mary Jane Shepley occupied the old saloon just south of Brent's new digs.

Brent laughed as if he was about to start a new adventure and left them to drive to the store and unload his gear.

Gavin watched Brent a moment or two, then asked Deedra, "Met anyone else here yet?"

"No. Tell me about the people living in that old hotel. They sound fascinating."

"Better yet. Let's walk over there and I'll introduce you. Those young people sure do hate to have their creativity interrupted. Better talk to them before they get started for the day."

Deedra laughed, recalling her own frustration at interruptions when she was writing. She had to take two steps to each one of Gavin's to keep up with his long strides.

Grinning with amusement, Gavin slowed so Deedra didn't have to scurry to keep up with him.

The hotel was a three-storied structure with wooden balustrades bordering large balconies which ran the length of the hotel overlooking Frontier Street.

Gavin yelled, "Anyone up in there?"

There was a sound of footsteps, then a squeak as the battered looking front door opened. A dark eyed youth with an extremely thin face and straight black hair combed back from a pronounced widow's peak opened the door. When Deedra looked into his dark eyes, she instantly recognized a miscreant whose thoughts most assuredly operated on a sub-normal level. This young man wasn't a conformist and was quite possibly of an occult mien.

"Yes?" the young man asked.

"Police, Derryck. We have some questions," Gavin said.

The young man opened the door wider and motioned for them to come in. The room Deedra and Gavin entered was the hotel's lobby. Long narrow stairs led upward, repaired here and there with new spindles or rough lumber causing the old part to look fragile. The room was clean, the furniture a creation of boxes and old lumber that managed to break up the desolation of an otherwise harsh-looking room. The table, made of planks placed across ore bins, was barren, though Deedra suspected they ate there, even though at the moment there was no sign of breakfast preparations.

Deedra heard movements from the upper reaches, and several heads suddenly appeared over the banisters. Then there was a scramble as young people raced down the wooden stairs, the echo of it rattling the windows, and resounding around and around the old lobby.

Two young women, fresh-faced, unsophisticated, dressed in jeans and men's shirts, were followed by two young men who loped down the stairs. One was heavyset with wide hazel eyes and light brown hair. The other, taller, more trim, had blue eyes and dark blonde hair.

Gavin looked at Derryck Evans, the young man who had opened the door for them, expecting him to introduce his friends. He did not, causing a moment of strained silence. Then the sheriff introduced them.

Valerie Penrose was an artist with honey-blonde hair and delicate features. Shelly Muldoon was a brownish-blonde with Irish features and that friendly Irish freshness to her looks. When Deedra learned that she wrote mysteries, she took a deep interest in the young woman.

Mark Saylen, the sturdy looking man, was a science fiction writer, and Deedra perceived that he took guff off no man. He had a long jaw line and unsuspected dimples that flashed when he smiled. His hazel eyes missed nothing, and at that moment they raked over Deedra with critical appraisement. Evidently she met with his approval.

Zach Johnson was a contrast. Tall, slim, with blue-violet eyes that held the tranquility of the sea and that faraway look of the artist. Deedra sensed that he was extremely talented, noting the sensitive face and his shapely hands.

Gavin had told her that Rhonda Adams had bossed the others about, and that she was the one who had arranged for the group to rent the old hotel. He also told her that the others were financially dependent on Rhonda. They hadn't liked her and had avoided her as much as possible.

"Frank Shundo said you worked for the *Daily Spokesman* newspaper?" Derryck Evans inquired, his dark eyes ferreting her thoughts.

"Yes. I heard about this old fossil dig and got my editor to assign me to the story. I don't often get a glimpse of such old bones," she laughed hoping the young people would join in. Mark and Shelley grinned. The others evidently didn't find her funny.

She met Derryck's smoldering gaze, a stare that was not friendly. Indeed, it was definitely hostile. What did Derryck fear from her? Or was it just the interruption of his work, the annoyance of having another stranger around?

She glanced around, noting the alertness etched on the young people's features. They seemed to sense that her purpose in being there was probably official and they were disturbed by it.

Beside her, Gavin stirred restively.

Since no one spoke, Deedra babbled nervously on. "I was really surprised to learn that there was a murder here. I went to school with Gregg Dancer and Frank Shundo, a couple of people from your town. I'm also acquainted with Mary Jane Shepley, although I can't say we are friends. Actually though, I'm just a rock-hound and amateur gemologist, and I just couldn't resist getting a look at that old mixosaur. They say the bones are agatized. Carnelian agate, and partly of opalized replacement. Have any of you seen them?" Deedra knew the bones were not opalized, and hoped for a reaction.

The two young women nodded, though it was

obvious that none of them knew the difference between agatized and opalized rock. She noted a quirk of humor in Gavin's eyes, though he didn't say anything.

The talk reverted to the weather and how long the group had lived in the old hotel. There were hesitant invitations to see their studios and to admire how they had fixed up the old building for their individual needs.

Deedra followed them around the second floor where the writers had set up studios, leaving the third floor to the artists because of its advantageous north light and view of the mountains and valley. All the rooms had access to the balconies.

Mark Saylen, the tough science fiction writer, had taken over the first three rooms. It was filled with books and pamphlets and writing materials. Sci-fi posters smothered the rough walls. The room where he kept his typewriter and actually did his writing was just off the bedroom where Deedra saw an unmade sleeping bag and clothes piled here and there. Above the typewriter stand, which was actually an old door scavenged from one of the ancient shanties, was a star chart. Planets, stars, and asteroids were listed there. A huge moon map and its phases was to his right, a list of constellations and their stars was placed in front of the typewriter. With different colored flair pens Mark had underlined the large craters on the moon map, all the places named Mare. Emphasis was placed on the crater Copernicus, as if he were writing about it. Books on astronomy were placed on plank shelves. All the furniture was constructed of materials found in and around the ghost town.

There was a half-typed manuscript on the typewriter stand. On crude shelves were ballpoint pens, paper, carbon paper, and bond paper. Mark had even decorated the wide windows with curtains made from a sheet and painted with stars and rocket ships.

The view from one of Mark's windows faced the alley between Frontier Street and Bridge Street to the south of the hotel. It was named Boothill Alley for the cemetery located on the slopes just above it. The ridge rose jaggedly behind the cemetery and cut North Ledge off from the south. Deedra could see the broken tombstones, and realized the cemetery was an ideal atmosphere for fantasy writing, though more suited to Derryck Evans' temperament. Deedra felt instant rapport with Mark Saylen and was anxious to read some of his writing which was created in the old-fashioned way. No electricity here.

Mark had watched Deedra, noted that she had approved of his "studio," that she saw all the advantages to a writer, was aware of its tranquility and lack of distraction. Mark noted her envy at his lack of responsibility and was pleased by it. She grinned at him. Mark nodded with satisfaction knowing that only another writer could appreciate the environment. It was evidently important to him to have Deedra's approval, knowing that most of the world wouldn't understand his need for space and quiet and privacy.

The next three rooms were Shelley Muldoon's. The first one they entered had walls lined with makeshift bookshelves braced by parts of old mining equipment. It contained a set of encyclopedias, volumes of old classics, books on law enforcement and law, reference books on a variety of subjects. All the writer's special books were there. Copies of *The Writer* magazine were stacked in a broken barrel turned on its side to form a magazine rack.

The room where Shelley worked contained large windows overlooking Bridge Street and the road leading into North Ledge. Shelley could see anyone entering the old ghost town from North San Juan. A glance out the window showed Deedra that the North San Juan road was cut through a narrow canyon of mica schist and various porphyry boulders. Few trees grew there, though Shelley's studio was shaded in the afternoon so the view didn't create the illusion of aridity as it might have otherwise.

Mismatched curtains hung at windows though they weren't unpleasing to the eye. Her typewriter was on a collapsible typewriter stand. Upright crates on each side of the stand held paper and other writing materials. A thesaurus, a copy of *Bartlett's Quotations,* and a medical dictionary sat beside her typewriter.

Shelley's bedroom walls, like her workroom walls, were covered with pictures, most of them cut from magazines. There were many seascapes, and over Shelley's sleeping bag was an original painting, possibly done by one of the artists here. Like Mark's room, Shelley's had only the necessities of life and nothing more. Deedra thought again how little artists and writers needed of the world's material things. Complete happiness was a state of mind. The world of the big city seemed to mean nothing to these young people who appeared to shun the crass scramble to the top that went with the modern version of success.

Rhonda Adams's rooms were at the far northern end with several rooms separating her studio from Shelley's. Unlike the others, Rhonda's rooms were harsh: all loud colors, none of the soothing blues and green tones found elsewhere. Lurid posters lined the walls giving the rooms lewd overtones. On shelves of planed lumber were copies of books written by X.R. Adams. The titles were erotic and shocking in theme. Her typewriter sat on a large desk surrounded by writing materials.

Deedra wished she could see in the drawers. She suspected they probably held sexual objects. Rhonda's ghost seemed to scamper about the room, gleeful in creating shock and disapproval. Deedra glanced at Gavin and saw the flicker of disgust in his eyes. Although he had searched this room right after the discovery of the body, he hadn't volunteered any information about what he had found there to Deedra. She had no idea the type of person the victim had been, or appeared to have been. Deedra knew she would have to ferret out a lot more information about the victim from talking to the others she lived with.

As they climbed the stairs to the third floor, Deedra gazed at the wide balcony and wondered if anyone famous had ever sat there watching the town's activities.

Zach Johnson's were the first three rooms on the top floor, his studio facing north. From wide lofty windows was a view of the whole town of North Ledge with the exception of the saloon where the Shepley's lived, and the store Brent had taken over.

Deedra could see the Catholic Church where she bunked and far out off the old stage road was a newly traveled trail which forded the creek and wended its way up the mountainside.

"Is that the way to the mixosaur dig?" Deedra asked.

"Yes," Zach answered with a gentle smile.

Deedra looked about the studio with unusual interest. It wasn't often she was privy to an artist's abode. The walls were covered with paintings of the ocean, a few done in the French Impressionist mode with cool pastel colors of non-peopled landscapes. On the easel set up in the north light was the likeness of the scene out the window. A copy of Paul Gaugin's *Woman and Mango,* one of Claude Monet's *Rouen Cathedral, West Facade, Sunlight,* hung between the artist's own paintings. Sail cloth painted with ocean scenes hung at the windows. The room was extremely neat. Deedra saw talent in the paintings; saw the intuitive grasp of perspective, the skilled use of color, the knowledge of dimension that projected depth into his art.

"Zach, have you ever heard of the Kevin Gates Art School?"

"Yes. It's my ambition to go there. I just can't afford it now."

"Kevin is a friend of mine. Perhaps you'll let me send him one of your seascapes. You might be eligible for a scholarship."

Zach smiled, excitement sparkling his eyes. He was so stunned by Deedra's offer that he could only nod quickly masking the tears of appreciation.

They tramped down the hall to Valerie Penrose's studio. It was so completely different from all the others that Deedra gasped.

Everything bespoke of the girl's daintiness and shy personality. Her paintings were modernistic though, impressionistic, and there were portraits of other young people living in the hotel. Several copies of Van Gogh's paintings decorated the rough-planked walls which

Valerie had covered with white butcher paper. She had created a bookshelf of crates, covered it with white butcher paper and then painted impressionistic designs of artists and writers at work.

Valerie's bedroom contained an old mattress on which she had placed her sleeping bag. Real lace curtains hung at the windows. A large mirror was on the far wall above a makeshift dressing table covered with cosmetics. Here, too, the walls were covered with white butcher paper then painted in pastel tones of green. It was, thought Deedra, like stepping into a soft green meadow, out of the harshness of reality. She smiled to herself, suspecting that Valerie was the one who suffered the most from the deprivations of their primitive lifestyle.

At the south end was Derryck Evans' studio. Deedra experienced a chilly premonition and steeled herself for an unpleasant experience.

Derryck threw open the door. His eyes were sparking with a mischievous leer and a smile quirked the corners of his mouth.

Deedra gasped as she stepped inside where a huge surrealistic painting depicting weird half-animal, half-humans in acts of murder, rape, and cannibalism, hung on the far wall. It hit the eye with savage fierceness.

Everywhere surrealistic paintings of hobgoblins, alien-world creatures, splattered the walls. It was like fierce graffiti, anger spawned forth in a froth of color. Deedra was even more shocked by the painting on Derryck's easel depicting the cemetery where ghosts and zombies arose among the tombstones with surrealistic dimensions.

Her heart hammered. She breathed deeply as she backed from the room. The hallway seemed drab and very dull after her visit to Derryck's sanctum.

Even Gavin's face took on grim lines of uneasiness and evident suspicion. He probably thought Derryck capable of all the Stygian shades of life.

Deedra noted that Valerie's studio was as far from Derryck's as it was possible for her to get.

Derryck glanced at Deedra with a gleeful look that told her he was amused at having shocked her. His eyes held a strange gleam of triumph and dark warning. He laughed in a derisive manner, then slammed back into his studio. His wicked laughter echoed down the hallways as they went down the stairs.

Deedra was glad the trip downstairs disguised her shudder.

THREE

DEEDRA STUDIED Gavin's reaction to Derryck with a mixture of amusement and uneasiness. She was aware that she was much more knowledgeable about art than Gavin. She also suspected that Derryck was not quite right in the head. No one painted surrealism all the time. Derryck was like the psychologist she had once met who smiled in the same smirking way and had finally been sent to an institution for terrorizing people with psychological tricks. Only the abnormal really wanted to frighten people constantly. Others might play pranks, but they lacked the heavy overtones Derryck had created in his art. She wondered which of the black arts he practiced, and controlled another shudder as they descended the stairs.

Outside they were just in time to see the Shepleys drive off toward the dig followed by the three scientists in an equipment-loaded Jeep. They all wore African safari hats as if they were headed for some distant place.

Brent walked across the street to join them, sending Deedra a glance meaning, "Tell me later." Instead he asked, "You want to follow them up to the dig?"

"Yes. Stop at the church so I can get my gear."

"I've some reports to attend to," Gavin said, "I'll see you two later." He waved them away.

DEEDRA ENJOYED the feeling of freedom and breathed deeply the clean mountain air as they drove up the mountainside. She was slightly relieved to get away from North Ledge, and knew that it stemmed from the sight of Derryck's paintings, the glimpse she'd had of his soul. She secretly suspected that the young people at the hotel had protected Valerie and Shelley from Rhonda's lechery and Derryck's kookiness.

Brent was silent as they drove up the old stage road and forded Jackson Creek. They climbed constantly cutting through brush and around boulders.

Deedra told of her impressions of the artists' studios while she bounced around on the seat and clung to the door handle.

"Do you think Derryck killed Rhonda Adams?" Brent asked when they reached a less difficult stretch of the makeshift road.

She glanced at the old mine tailings dotting the slopes on each side, the deserted mine shafts boring into the mountainsides, the scant vegetation limp under the summer heat. "I don't know. I've just met him. I think Derryck's a fraud. He gets a kick out of shocking people, but his delving into that kind of art all the time is not beneficial to his mental health. He might not be capable of killing anyone; he may work all that kind of dark emotion out on canvas. It may be a catharsis for him. Rhonda was knifed in the back, and I'm not sure Derryck would do that. I think he would want to scare her first, let her see the knife slashing down on her."

Deedra paused waiting for Brent to comment. He did not. "Now, Gregg's ex-wife, Mary Jane Shepley, is quite capable of such a killing. Especially if Gregg led her to believe he was interested in Rhonda. Mary Jane is dangerous. Getting Gregg blamed for a murder she committed would suit her just fine. Knowing Mary Jane, I suspect she resents not being able to control Gregg anymore."

Brent laughed. "Tell me about Gregg Dancer. Old beau of yours?"

"No, just a friend. We had a crush on each other during our teen years. He's a very intelligent guy, a geologist consultant for major mining companies like Anaconda Copper. It's such a waste to kill off that kind of training and know-how, and that's what will happen if he's arrested for Rhonda's murder. He has an extremely likable personality. Not the kind of person to get mixed up in anything scandalous. Sort of a shy guy, really."

Brent nodded. "What about Frank Shundo? What's his training exactly?"

"He's head engineer for the Sierra Mining Company. I don't know much about him anymore. I haven't seen him since we graduated from high school. Until last night, that is. He was a trustworthy, popular student, and I don't think his character has changed. He's third generation Japanese-American."

"How do you think Gregg's initials got scratched into that knife handle?"

"I think that whoever did this is trying to implicate Gregg. I don't think Gregg had any previous acquaintance with Rhonda. People seldom kill strangers unless paid to do it, or they're just plain psycho. Gavin is leaning towards Gregg as the main suspect. I'm afraid he is going to be arrested for murder."

"You don't think he killed Rhonda?"

"No." She didn't tell Brent that Gregg and Frank just

weren't the murdering type..Who really could tell who was going to commit a murder and who wouldn't? It was just her intuition that told her Gregg didn't do it, and that Frank wouldn't do it either.

"Did Gavin say they questioned all the amateurs that were up here at the dig? I understand the place has been overrun with them since word of the fossil find got out."

"Yes. The D.A. did interviews but there were no standout leads. We know how Rhonda was killed, where and when it happened, but not why. The motive isn't clear. Gregg is here in an official capacity to record the geologic strata of the dig. He never met Rhonda Adams before arriving here. At least there is no evidence of that. The fact that a mixosaur bone was found beside her dead body is what ties her to the dig and those concerned with it. Frank Shundo didn't have anything to do with the dig; he's looking at old mines. Of course, Derryck Evans could have slipped a cog and lived out one of his fantasies."

"I don't think that's a motive, it's more like a dark impulse. Derryck might have killed her from some kind of sexual motive," Brent suggested, shrugging.

The roadway to the site was one of the most difficult to traverse that Deedra had ever seen. She knew that the scientists were not going to improve it either. The fewer people around their dig, the better they liked it. When they rode over the steep slope they could see the Shepleys and the others gathered around the dig. One man held a clipboard. As they got closer, Deedra saw that it was Gregg Dancer. The others were busy with shovels and picks. Evidently they were removing the overburden from the quarry; otherwise they would not have risked using such heavy tools.

"Let's see if we can trap a killer, Deedra," Brent murmured as they made their way down the steep gully, a gully flanked on each side with millions of years of volcanic deposits.

The scientists and Mary Jane Shepley looked up as Brent and Deedra approached. Deedra saw surprise on Mary Jane's face when she recognized Deedra. She looked away long enough to compose herself, and when she faced Deedra again, her emotions were masked behind a haughty calmness. If Mary Jane had killed Rhonda, she would never allow the guilt to show on her face.

Deedra wondered hōw much grief she felt over the divorce from Gregg. They had been married several years—there surely must be residue of that relationship between them.

She glanced at the scientists and found no welcome in their taciturn expressions. Instead, there was ill-concealed resentment at having their work observed and intruded upon.

"Hi," Deedra greeted as she and Brent walked up to the edge of the pit. She saw vertebrae bones and remnants of large, sharp, conical teeth with a ring of bony plates lying beside it. They had excavated an entire mixosaur complete with its biconcave vertebral. It resembled the large ichthyosaurus' long shark-like snout, though it looked more like the modern day whale.

Brent quickly photographed the mixosaur before anyone could object.

Deedra put them at ease, ignoring Mary Jane as if

she didn't recognize her. "I see the mixosaur is not agatized replacement. Have you found any of the bones agatized?"

A youngish man about thirty-five years old grinned. "A few. Chalcedony mostly. Lots of silica here mixed with the old ocean sand. It's an uplifted block that moved the mixosaur bones upward over the eons. This is all Mesozoic strata with left-over Triassic fossils. Lots of ammonites, trilobites, and gastropod here for the mixosaurus to feed on." He pointed to a pile of ammonites which resembled fossil snails.

Deedra observed several trilobites, guessing at their weight. "About 180 million years old then?"

"Yes," the man laughed. "I'm Steven Robbins, I teach paleontology, and specialize in Ichthyology. Have you seen the Nevada deposit?"

"Yes," Deedra replied. "I'm an old rock-hound and amateur gemologist. This is my friend, Brent Larsen. I thought I'd get a look at this old fossil site. It's thrilling! When I saw the Berlin, Nevada, site near Gabbs, I was very young. Those bones were agatized as I recall."

"Yes. This quarry here has several animals, perhaps more than the Berlin, Nevada, site. We think there are several right here in this gully, though our initial investigation hasn't turned up any more other than right here. This is a geologic phenomenon."

Deedra glanced up the mountainside. "Any other fossils?"

"Not that we've uncovered. And just here," he pointed to the pit, "is the only place we've located the mixosaur. It doesn't seem to extend into the mica schist or the porphyry. I'd like to see what's under that old mountain, though," he pointed to a cliff at the far right next to Quartz Mountain.

Deedra laughed. "I'll bet you would. With a name like Quartz Mountain you could expect to find all kinds of interesting things." The other two men had stopped work and were regarding her with more respect. Gregg Dancer was grinning as though he had just won some kind of contest. The shorter man was Dr. Kurt Von Kraus, a leading authority in the physical sciences, whose name she instantly recognized. She had read his papers on theories of prehistoric life, and its effect on modern day life. He had, she knew, been consulted by the most eminent scholars about his theories of life in outer space.

The other scientist was a tall, broad-shouldered man with dark eyes and thinning gray hair. Deedra also recognized him, the famous Dr. John Drake, anthropologist and archaeologist.

Actually, she mused, Gregg Dancer was the only one really qualified to record the geologic strata since that was his specialty. Then she remembered that Alfred Shepley was also a geologist, though he was not doing the recording. Gregg was writing in his notebook and ignoring Alfred.

Alfred, she gathered, was not a happy man. He was like a third person on a date. He was young, brash, aggressive in a pitiful way, and obviously overwhelmed by his colleagues. He had dark, curly hair and dark brown eyes that held a half-concealed contempt for her. The look he gave Brent was one of anger and resentment.

Deedra studiously ignored him, knowing that would make him angrier than any words she could utter. Alfred

Shepley was the type who needed the spotlight constantly, felt hurt and insecure if he wasn't the center of attention. Since Mary Jane was of that ilk, she wondered whether their marriage was compatible, with each seeking to outdo the other. How Mary Jane could marry a man like Alfred Shepley after having been married to Gregg Dancer was a mystery.

Brent took lots of pictures, many of the scientists, which seemed to please them despite their attitude toward interruptions.

Deedra continued her conversation with Steven Robbins, an exceedingly friendly personality. "Is that mixosaur descended from the ichthyosaur or vice versa?"

"No," he replied. "It's just another ichthyosaur type. They all lasted about 100 million years. These here evidently died of lung collapse and sank into the primordial ooze just like those at the Nevada site. They were all the largest creatures of their time."

Deedra hesitated then asked, "How was the site discovered?"

"A rock-hound notified the university."

"Did you know that I grew up in the same neighborhood as Gregg Dancer?" Deedra remarked in a casual way.

Gregg suddenly looked uncertain, as if she had said something he did not care to have known.

It was as if a stick of dynamite had been thrown into their excavation. Everyone stopped what they were doing and stared at her. A wall of hostility was instantly there. They turned to Gregg with instant suspicion. Did they think Gregg had invited her there for some devious purpose?

"I also went to school with Frank Shundo, but I had no idea they were up here when my editor sent me here to get a story. It's a pleasure to see you again, Gregg. I talked with Frank a moment last night."

FOUR

IT WAS AS IF EVERYONE at the dig was involved in the child's game of statues, and was waiting for Deedra to say, "May I?"

Dr. Steven Robbins was the first to recover, inquiring in a quiet voice, "Is that right? Did Gregg invite you up here?"

"No. I haven't seen him in several years. Until last night, that is. I was sent here by my editor to do a story on the dinosaur find as well as the recent murder up here. I know a lot of people here it turns out; Mary Jane is also an old acquaintance of mine. She used to live in my neighborhood."

Alfred glanced with alarm at Mary Jane.

"Yes, I know Frank Shundo and Gregg Dancer. So what?" Mary Jane looked at Alfred who was glaring at her.

This stopped further questioning just as Mary Jane had intended.

Deedra sighed. The same old Mary Jane.

To relieve the tension, Deedra asked Dr. Robbins, "Does the mixosaur have a terminal fin and paddle-like limbs?"

"Yes. It's a true ichthyosaur. Straight backbone, though. This old fellow here," Dr. Robbins pointed to the fossil skeleton, "lacks much of what was found at the Holzmaden, Southern Germany, site. Just the bones have been preserved which wouldn't tell us all we want to know without the ammonites, and the information from the Nevada site. That large fin on his back acted as a keel when he swam. See there, the limbs even have finger and toe bones. It's another Stenopterygius-type, all right."

"I understand the mixosaur is sort of a mixture of the old crocodile and a fish creature?" Deedra ventured.

"Yep. Only the iguanodon of modern day is anything like the reptile part of it. The ancient Coelacanth fish is possibly a remote descendent of the fish part. They're still catching Coelacanths, and they're bigger than the fossil forms. I went to the Comoros Islands to see them. Interesting specimens, have an ancient out-of-this-world look."

The other scientists including Alfred Shepley went on with their work. He regarded Deedra with suspicion and seemed uneasy in her presence.

Brent stopped taking photos and watched something on the north slope of Quartz Mountain. She followed his gaze and saw Frank Shundo searching about on the tailings of an old gold mine. The discarded quartz crystals glittered like jewels in the bright sunlight.

Brent nodded to Deedra. "Let's go and let these people get on with their work."

They started climbing toward the old mine and never knew if Frank Shundo saw them and deliberately avoided them, or if he just didn't find anything at the old mine site and moved on. When they reached the mine near the top of Quartz Mountain, he had vanished as if he had been a mirage.

"Damn funny. He was here just a few minutes ago.

How could he have disappeared so fast?" Brent glanced around the slope, a look of frustration pulling his mouth into a frown.

Deedra wondered if Brent thought Frank had something about his work here that he didn't want the media to know about.

"There might be another mine shaft that we can't see from here." Deedra knew how deceptive mountain landscapes were, knew that deep gullies existed that couldn't be seen from a distance. That Frank Shundo had disappeared was not remarkable to her.

"Look, Brent. These crystals are nearly perfect. There must have been a trace of silver with the gold in this mine. See that silvery shine on the crystals? Gold and silver are often found together, and then it's called 'electrum.' Look here, a quartz crystal shaped like a rose. This one has drusy quartz stained with iron." Deedra placed the specimens in her pack and hurried after Brent who had wandered inside an old mine shaft.

The shaft seemed sturdy enough, the timbers overhead still intact, but old mines were treacherous and Deedra cautioned, "Don't go in there, Brent! Those old timbers could give way with the least noise. It's been over a hundred years since some of them were placed there."

Brent stopped, shining the beam of his flashlight into the dark shaft.

Deedra was aware of his disappointment, but Brent wasn't foolish. He wasn't about to enter a mine that might collapse around him, no matter how badly he wanted to see what was there. She knew that he thought Frank Shundo was hiding in there somewhere. But knowing how cautious Frank was, Deedra didn't think he'd venture in. It was cool in the shaft though, and Deedra shivered.

They caught sight of Frank on the north slope of Mercury Mountain. Brent was rather chagrined about thinking Frank was deliberately hiding.

"You know, Brent, I saw some mineral samples in Gregg's place with traces of copper in them. They say there isn't any copper up here, but it seems strange that Gregg would bring samples of copper here with him when he is officially here to record the mixosaur site strata."

Brent frowned. "Perhaps not. We don't know where he went during these last few months. Some mining company might have sent him or even given them to him for analysis. It isn't unusual for a geologist to have all sorts of mineral samples and carry them about with him."

"I suppose you're right." Deedra paused. "Let's sit here on these old mine tailings and watch where Frank goes."

Frank Shundo headed toward an old mining operation near the top of Mercury Mountain. Deedra could still see the switchback trail leading up the mountain where supplies had been hauled to the mines by pack burros and teams of oxen. Frank Shundo didn't follow the trail; instead he climbed straight up toward the mine. The tailings were dull and didn't glitter in the sunlight like those she and Brent sat on.

"You know, Brent, there are twelve suspects. All of them have been up here for several weeks. Gavin hasn't been able to find out if there were any violent quarrels or fights during that time. Mary Jane and Rhonda could have carried on quite a feud. Frank might have had a disagreement with Rhonda. Any of the young people could have motives, especially if Rhonda was as evil as her rooms and writing indicate." She paused, "Gavin said Gregg was in love with Valerie, and Rhonda was in love with Gregg, and Mary Jane was jealous. Usually the motives for murder are greed, lust, hatred, self-protection, and revenge. It's likely that her murderer was motivated by anger and hatred. I doubt that greed enters into it."

"We need to find out if Gregg or Frank knew Rhonda from college or somewhere. If not, it certainly weakens their motives," Brent replied.

"Still," remarked Deedra, "it is curious that a mixosaur bone was placed beside her dead body unless it has some significance. Was it put there later by someone who wanted to implicate one of the scientists? Did Rhonda drop it? And if so, how did she have possession of it?"

"I wondered where your thoughts were taking you, Deedra. I suspect that Mark and Zach had their hands full keeping Rhonda from trying to get Shelley and Valerie involved in her pornographic art."

Deedra jumped, startled. "You really think it was as bad as that?"

"Yes. I could be wrong, but I have read a few things by X.R. Adams. They are shocking and steamy. I couldn't see a woman writing that stuff, and am surprised that it was."

"So you read her stuff, eh?" Deedra grinned, giving him an oblique glance. "I didn't think you were into erotica."

"I'm not, but I was curious after being told about some of the things she wrote by colleagues in Sweden."

"Ah, Sweden, land of the free," Deedra sighed.

"Yeah," Brent grinned. "Frank has reached those old mines. What exactly would he be looking for there?"

"Test samples from the tailings, tracings of minerals. I'm not sure what he's really looking for, though. Mining companies send men into these old mining fields. It's a known fact that the miners of the 1800s didn't recognize anything but gold and silver, and sometimes not even that."

Brent laughed. "Most of them couldn't read, Deedra."

"Well, there could be something of value in those old dredgings. Today's technology and manufacturing use a variety of minerals."

They watched as Frank picked up samples of rock, occasionally placing one in his pack sack. He carried a geologist's crack hammer, and sometimes broke specimens into smaller pieces. Evidently he found something interesting because he took out a notebook and jotted an entry in it. It was speculation, of course, for they really couldn't see what he was doing for sure.

"Let's climb to the top of the mountain so I can get a picture of North Ledge from above," Brent suggested.

The climb wasn't difficult, though the high elevation and thin air caused them heavy breathing. The view was extraordinary, the breeze cool and almost chilly. The scientists looked like ants moving about the mountainside.

Brent shot the ghost town from several angles then laid the camera aside and took her into his arms.

"I know we haven't been dating much lately, and I know you still carry a torch for Deke Thomas, but he is never going to give up his bachelor status. You know that, and I know that."

"And you can be persuaded to change your status?" Deedra challenged.

"I might," he stared into her eyes. "I have been

married, it just didn't work. Women don't like it when men traipse all over the world on news stories, and they never know when they are going to return, or if they will. You know how dangerous some of our assignments are. However, I have received the word that I may not have to take any more overseas assignments. How about that? Does that make me a more interesting fellow?"

Deedra gave him a kiss that showed her interest more than words could have done.

"Careful, Deedra, Frank can see us, and I saw Gavin with his binoculars earlier." Seeing her hesitation he said, "We'll go into the mine shaft, just far enough to be out of sight. I don't want to kiss you in front of an audience either."

Brent took Deedra's hand and led her into the mine shaft where half an hour earlier Frank Shundo had been searching. Even as she allowed Brent to lead her there and was excited by him, she also wondered what it was that Frank was hoping to find there earlier.

Later, outside the dark mine shaft, Deedra visually traced Jackson Creek as it wended its way along the base of the mountain under the bridges of North Ledge to finally vanish on the far side of Boothill Range. It was, she mused, like being at the end of the world with the residents of North Ledge the sole survivors, a removal of civilization.

"Look, Brent!"

Frank Shundo had fallen. He had started down the mountain, and then suddenly threw up his arms as if startled by something. They watched breathlessly until they saw him get up, brush off his clothing, glance back toward the mine, and then stalk down the mountain as if angry or disgusted about something.

After exploring the mountain top and looking at several old mines, they started the long descent to Brent's 4-wheel rig. The scientists didn't look up as they marched past the diggings. The scientists were probably glad Deedra and Brent didn't stop to talk. They were most likely afraid they might have to stop their work and perhaps answer more questions.

However, Mary Jane watched them closely as they passed, her eyes slanted in contemplation. Deedra knew what she was thinking about which caused Deedra to blush.

THEY DROVE OVER the bridge into North Ledge just as someone raced around the corner of the store Brent called "home" and vanished into Dead Man's Alley.

"Could you tell who that was?" Brent demanded.

"No. Just running legs wearing jeans. Couldn't tell if it was a man or a woman." Deedra tried to recall something familiar about the person but didn't know the people in town well enough yet to recognize anyone.

Brent looked about in his place for signs of search and seizure. "Nothing seems to be missing," he said in a puzzled voice.

It was an interesting old building with the old store's counter and shelving still intact. She could almost see the old miners lined up at the counter, now worn thin, for the whiskey that warmed and sustained them in times of discouragement.

"Let's find Gavin."

Brent strode off toward the saloon with Deedra scurrying to keep up. Brent was definitely not the genteel type, and she tried not to give the impression that she had to run to keep up with him. Perhaps, she thought resentfully, women should still walk ten paces behind their men. Then laughed at herself. Brent treated her like he would any other reporter, making no distinction between male and female. Everyone had to fend for themselves.

They found Sheriff Blair eating lunch and reading the autopsy report on Rhonda Adams.

"Was Rhonda killed at the time you suspected, Sheriff?" Deedra inquired. She noted that Frank's abode across the street seemed deserted. It would, she mused, have been very easy for Frank to have gone into the alley, killed Rhonda, and then have slipped back across the street to his house. It would have taken only a minute or two. It would have been just as easy for Gregg, or any of the young people living in the hotel. "Any of the people here could have killed her. It would have only taken a minute or two," Deedra remarked.

"Yep," Gavin replied. "Rhonda was killed about 9:00, give or take a few minutes. I'm sure it was later. After dark, that is. The killer would have been seen if it had been earlier, and the young people would have stumbled over her body when they returned from the swimming hole. Before nightfall everyone seems to have moved about in their usual activities. After dark, no one seems to know where anyone else was for sure. At least that's what they say. Under cover of darkness, anyone could have gone into that alley, killed Rhonda, and left without having been observed."

"Do you think she had an appointment to meet anyone?"

"I'm not sure. The alley is an unlikely place for a

meeting. I think the killer just sneaked up behind her and
Rhonda didn't know what hit her. I think the killer made
certain he wasn't seen either entering or leaving the
alley, though there is the possibility that Alfred and
Mary Jane might have been on their front porch at the
time. They are both very vague about it."

"And no real motive for either of them?"

"Just that old fossil bone. It's another reason the
District Attorney thinks that Gregg Dancer is guilty.
Gregg could have obtained that bone easily enough,
and in the dark might have dropped it, and not had time
to retrieve it."

"Gregg isn't stupid, Gavin. He wouldn't have killed
Rhonda with a knife that had his own initials on it and left
clues pointing to himself," Deedra said in a firm voice.

Gavin gave her a deep look, but didn't answer, aware
she knew that he didn't think Gregg was guilty either.

"You're sure she was killed in the alley, not moved
there?"

"Yes. There weren't any signs that the body had been
dragged through the dust, and she was a big woman. I
think she'd be too big for someone to carry on their own.
Mark Saylen might have been able to manage it—he's
big enough. But he doesn't seem to have motive enough
to be bothered. It takes planning and guts to commit
murder. I don't think Mark would take that much time
away from his writing. He admits that he detested the
woman, that she was not a real author, but simply a hack
churning out filth for the unintelligent. All the young
people said she really wasn't an artist, that she was cor-
rupted and greedy. I'm sure she worried them. I think
Valerie Penrose was even afraid of her."

"Yes, I can understand that," Deedra replied. "Can I see the weapon?"

"It's with the District Attorney. I've got a photo of it, though." Gavin handed her an enlarged photo of the knife.

It was a large hunting knife, the kind sportsmen carried in sheaths on their belts. Deedra had just purchased an almost identical one for her trip to North Ledge. The initials G.D. had been scratched into the hilt by a sharp object, probably another knife. There were faint lines on the hilt as if someone had marked it with a pencil. Deedra studied it with the uncanny sensation of looking at something important and not being able to see the significance of it. The knife was not unusual in any way. Practically every sporting goods store had them for sale. Only the initials had made it seem to be the property of Gregg Dancer. It could have belonged to anyone, and there was no real way to trace it. It wasn't new, and it had been wiped free of fingerprints.

"How many other knives like this are there in North Ledge, Gavin?" she asked.

"All the men have similar ones and by all accounts they still have them. The women claim they don't own any, but I suspect they had knives for protection, and didn't want anyone to learn of it."

"What was everyone doing the day Rhonda was killed?"

"The professors were up at the dig until after two P.M. Alfred and Mary Jane were up there also. It got too hot to work so they came back to North Ledge early. The scientists made some lab tests then just relaxed. Gregg hiked up Mica Mountain and Frank was on Mercury Mountain all that day. Alfred and Mary Jane took naps, and the hotel people said they just 'created' as usual with the exception of Rhonda, who sat on the hotel balcony most of the afternoon."

"Then Rhonda could have observed something that went on that afternoon. You can see all over North Ledge from up there."

"Yes," Gavin agreed. "She evidently saw Valerie go up Boothill Ridge in a round about way to meet Gregg. Since Rhonda was supposed to be in love with Gregg that must have made her furious. I gather she was a woman of quick temper and deep emotions. She may have argued with Gregg about it later. Gregg says he usually met Valerie away from North Ledge because he didn't want Mary Jane to learn about their relationship. Evidently she has the idea that she still has a say in Gregg's life."

"Steven Robbins says he went to Gregg's place, knocked on the door, and though Gregg wasn't home, went in and borrowed some books. Frank returned to his place for a few minutes then went back up on Mercury Mountain. District Attorney Narkett thinks Frank may have taken Gregg's knife at that time. No one saw him return to North Ledge later."

"Does he think Frank scratched Gregg's initials onto that knife hilt, or that he killed Rhonda?"

"He thinks Frank might have killed Rhonda."

"I thought his main suspect was Gregg?" Deedra sounded puzzled.

"It is, but he doesn't want to miss any clue."

"If," Deedra suggested, "Steven Robbins went into Gregg's place he could have taken the knife along with the books."

"Yes, I thought of that. The only hitch is that Gregg claims it is not his knife. He says he didn't have initials carved on it, and that the hilt was a different color, almost black. Gregg's knife could have been taken several days earlier, perhaps even a few weeks since he says he hasn't used it since he moved into that place."

Gavin consulted his notes. "They were all outside somewhere after supper time. It was an exceptionally warm evening, and everyone usually swam in the creek at night for their nightly bath. There is an old swimming hole behind the blacksmith shop. No one can swear where anyone else was after they left the swimming hole between 8:45 and 10:00. People moved about all evening because it was too warm inside the buildings. It was a dark evening, no moon or stars. We do know that Gregg swam in the river with Zach and Mark, and then walked with Shelley up the old stage road where she left him to go swimming with Valerie. Valerie was trying to get away from Rhonda. Rhonda didn't swim and seldom went to the places where the others were swimming. It was unusual that she did so that night. They all told me she usually sponge bathed further downstream. Anyway, after Shelley left Gregg, no one claims to have seen him that night. Steven Robbins found Rhonda the next morning when he stopped to give Gregg a ride up to the dig. Saw her lying facedown in the alley, so he shouted out the alarm."

"Then the other scientists could see Rhonda lying there in the alley from their car?" Deedra asked.

"No. At least the scientists all say not. Robbins called out to them and they hurried into the alley."

"Gregg followed them?"

"Yes. Though the others got there first. No chance of him leaving that fossil bone or taking the knife away."

"That means the killer snuck up on her. And you said there was no sign of struggle. Could the killer have mistaken Rhonda for someone else in the dark?"

"That's possible, of course. But it's my opinion that Rhonda was the target, that the killer got his intended victim."

"What motive aside from possibly the porno angle?" Deedra challenged.

"Jealousy seems the only likely one. Rhonda wasn't wealthy, however, that depends on how rich you have to be to be considered wealthy. She wasn't married to anyone that we have learned about. Maybe she learned something dangerous about the men working up at the dig. I honestly haven't found a good enough motive."

"Strange. Her reason for being up here isn't really clear either. She obviously didn't have rapport with the other young people, yet she arranged for them to live in that old hotel. Do you suppose she was in hiding?" Deedra suggested.

"Perhaps," Gavin answered in a doubtful tone. "That porn stuff might be the answer. It's real perversion, and what if she put the make on someone up here, learned something detrimental to their reputations? To a scientist, his reputation is a very important thing."

"That might mean that she had some connection with the criminal world. She had to have a market for that perverted art stuff," Brent suggested.

"I don't think anyone could have sneaked up here and snuffed her out, if that's what you mean, Brent. No one heard a vehicle, and the sound carries for miles up here.

No one gets in or out of North Ledge without being seen or heard."

Gavin sighed and scratched his head in a thoughtful way. "You see why it's all circumstantial evidence against Gregg Dancer? I don't believe he killed her, and he claims not to have known Rhonda before he arrived up here. So far we haven't proved that claim wrong. But the District Attorney will arrest him if we don't find the real killer, find proof that Gregg didn't murder her."

"Gavin, you know very well that anyone here could have committed it. Those initials could have been scratched into any knife."

"Yeah," Brent remarked. "We saw someone running from my place a while ago."

Gavin sat up, the chair legs hitting the wooden floor with a thump. "Who was it?"

"We couldn't tell. We know it wasn't the people up at the dig because we had just left them all there. That includes the Shepleys. It was most likely one of the young people from the hotel," Deedra remarked.

As a shadow crept across the floor, they looked up to see Derryck Evans standing in the doorway, the glitter of anger shining in his eyes.

FIVE

"Do you actually think any of us even care what you have in that old store?" Derryck asked in a scathing tone.

Brent answered in a voice geared to calm Derryck. "I didn't say we saw anyone inside the store. I said we saw someone alongside the store, and I think whoever it was ran down Dead Man's Alley. That someone didn't want us to see them. Now, I find that a strange action."

This topped whatever comment Derryck intended to make. He gestured in futility.

Gavin introduced him to Brent Larsen.

Deedra watched Brent's silent assessment of the surrealistic artist and wished that she could hear his thoughts.

Derryck turned to Gavin. "Did you find out when Rhonda was killed? Did you know that Mary Jane and Gregg had a terrible fight, a real lover's quarrel, early that evening?"

"Where did this take place?" Gavin's eyes narrowed, his jawline was taut.

Deedra knew he was wondering if Derryck was lying.

Derryck sent a sly glance at Deedra. "Actually, it was up near that old church."

"When?" Gavin's eyes had turned cold, his lips set in an uncompromising line.

"Just before dark. I heard them 'cause I was walking

along Jackson Creek, and I cut up behind the old church.
I didn't know they were there, didn't mean to eavesdrop."

"What did they say?" Gavin demanded.

Derryck gestured again as if it really didn't make any
sense. "Mary Jane was giving Gregg what-for, a real tongue
lashing. She said something like, 'You'll do as I say, Gregg,
or I'll make sure you never receive another consultant's
fee.' I don't know how she could have prevented Gregg
from getting work. That's what she said, though."

Deedra relaxed. It sounded so typical of Mary Jane that
she was certain the fight had actually taken place. Though
why would Mary Jane threaten Gregg? The divorce had
all been her idea, after all. Had she underestimated Alfred
Shepley's abilities? Had she now regretted the marriage,
and wanted Gregg back? Or had she demanded that Gregg
use his influence to help Alfred?

She glanced at Gavin, noted the warning flicker in
his eyes, and tacitly agreed to let Derryck think it meant
nothing. They both wondered if Derryck had told them
all he had heard.

Gavin put the thought into words. "That was all
they said?"

"It was all I heard." His eyes strayed around the room,
then after a moment of silence, "That's all I wanted to
say." He muttered something unintelligible under his
breath as he turned and strode back down Frontier Street.

Deedra watched as Derryck kicked up puffs of dust
in his wake, walking with his head bowed. He looked
neither right nor left as if contemplating some weighty
problem. What a strange person he was, she mused.

"He went straight to the hotel, Gavin. Do you think that
was true? Or was he just trying to divert our attention?"

"I think it's probably true. Though Derryck doesn't like Mary Jane, and might want to cause suspicion against her. I've seen him watch her with a sneer on his face." Gavin shook his head. "That Derryck is really an unusual person."

"Gavin, was there any other physical evidence at the crime scene besides that damn knife?" Brent inquired.

The sheriff leaned against the rough wall, the old chair tilting perilously. "I can't say for sure, Brent. I think Rhonda's things had been searched, though. We don't know how she left them or what she brought up here so we can't tell if anything is missing for sure. We don't know what was in her jeans pockets either. The killer might have taken something from her. Her writing notes were there. And unless one of the other writers wanted to break into the porn market, nothing was obviously missing."

"Did the writers look through her things?" Deedra frowned.

"Yes. Any reason they shouldn't have?" Gavin raised his eyebrows. "I wanted them to tell me if there was something there that most writers would not require or need."

"I guess not," Deedra drawled. What difference would it have made since any of them could have sneaked in there before the police arrived or just after she was murdered and removed anything that might have been incriminating.

"Gavin, may I borrow some of Rhonda's books? She may have left a clue in them."

Gavin's eyebrows went upward again as he studied Deedra, wanting to know what she was looking for. "Yes. They've already been checked for fingerprints. We only found Rhonda's. Don't mark on them. You think there might be something in her writing? Something to indicate that she was afraid of someone or trying to blackmail someone?"

"Perhaps. What I want to know is how did Rhonda get acquainted with these young people here? Who suggested that they move up here?"

"That's not strange really. They met at an art festival. Rhonda had put an ad on the bulletin board. She wanted five artists or writers to share the rent of that old hotel for six months. These were the five that applied."

She glanced at Brent and realized that he wanted to talk to Gavin, man to man. "I'm going to my place to get lunch. I'll see you fellows later," she said.

Stepping onto dusty Frontier Street was like walking onto an ancient movie set. The street was deserted, not even a lizard scurried in the deep dust. She glanced at the old Wells Fargo building and thought of a poem she had composed while writing a feature story on the famous Wells Fargo bandit, Black Bart. He had been called the poet laureate of the frontier, the PO8.

Under her breath she repeated the poem.

"Black Bart was known to one and all,
The white-masked man so slim and tall.
From every crime he walked away,
Bidding his victims all, "good day."
As PO8 his verse found fame,
And mystery still surrounds his name."

Her footsteps echoed on Stagecoach Bridge as she crossed Jackson Creek. In her imagination she envisioned a panting stage team racing across the bridge and amidst the dust and shouts halting in front of the old Wells Fargo station. *How the West was won,* she laughed to herself.

The door to the old church was ajar. Deedra distinctly remembered having shut it. Had even tested it to make certain no snakes or lizards could get in. She paused, wondering if someone was lurking inside. No sound intruded upon the stillness around the church.

Holding her breath, ready to run if danger threatened, she pushed the door open and allowed her eyes to get accustomed to the dim interior before entering.

Frank Shundo was seated on the floor leaning against the wall in back of the place where the lectern had stood.

"Frank! You gave me a scare. What are you doing here?"

"Deedra, I've got to talk to you alone. I didn't kill Rhonda. You've got to believe me. When they find out that she sneaked into my quarters at night, they'll think that I killed her. I'm not going to tell them unless they arrest Gregg, and then I won't keep quiet. I can't let that happen."

"What do you mean, Rhonda sneaked into your place at night?"

"Just that. I woke up one night and found her in bed with me. I didn't resist her advances. I guess I was flattered. She came back several times. I wasn't in love with her, you understand. And after awhile I didn't want her even around me anymore. She just wouldn't take no for an answer. We had a big argument the night before she was killed. She met me coming down Mercury Mountain, and wanted to know why I had put a lock on my door. I told her I didn't want to play around any more. She didn't like it, told me that if she wanted me to play around she had ways of making me."

"What did she mean by that?"

"I don't know. Just then we heard someone in the brush, and Rhonda went back to North Ledge."

"Did you see anyone?"

"No. Whoever was there didn't want to be seen. You know how easy it is to hide up here. Anyway, you've got to believe that I didn't kill her."

"Of course, I believe you. I don't think Gavin Blair believes you killed her either, and he doesn't believe that Gregg killed her. You know Gregg. He even hates to kill a snake."

"I know, but sooner or later they are going to find out that I knew Rhonda back in Los Angeles." Frank paused, seemed unable to go on for a moment, but finally continued. "I rented an apartment in the upstairs of a house Rhonda owned. We…ah…had a few encounters there. I didn't really like it, but it was hard to turn her away. Then I learned that she wrote porn when she showed me some of it. Real sick stuff. Then she said she had taken pictures while she and I were having sex. Said she wanted to see if the Japanese made love differently! It was disgusting and I got out of there. I never saw her again until she moved up here, and then I pretended not to know her. I thought she would take the hint that I didn't want to get mixed up with her again. I did threaten her about involving those young people in any of her porn schemes. She never mentioned any pictures of me. I think she had just said that to scare me. But you see how that makes me look? I haven't been able to bring myself to tell Gavin about it." Frank was definitely depressed.

"Oh, Frank, let's hope Gavin and the District Attorney don't find out about this. It may let Gregg off the hook, but it really puts you in jeopardy."

"You aren't going to tell him?" Frank looked sick.

"Not if you're truly innocent!" Deedra replied.

"Well, if things get too hot for Gregg, I'll tell the sheriff about it," Frank said.

Deedra nodded. Frank would never let Gregg down, they were truly friends.

"Does Gregg know about this?"

"I haven't told him. After I learned he had an affair with Rhonda that broke up his engagement to Shelley Muldoon, I just didn't say anything."

Despite Deedra's surprise, she asked, "What happened up here after Gregg arrived? Did you call him, how was he notified about the mixosaur find?"

"I called him from North San Juan right after it was discovered. Gregg and I have worked together several times on different explorations. He drove right up here after getting my call, got here three weeks ahead of those others!" Frank gestured toward the mixosaurus dig with disgust. "Gregg and I never lost touch after we graduated from college, and our work is practically in the same field. You remember how it was during high school? Gregg and me on the football team? I would never kill someone and let Gregg take the blame, Deedra!"

"Yes, I know. You've just got to keep a cool head and answer my questions. Did Mary Jane Shepley arrive right away?"

"No. Alfred Shepley sort of butted in on the scientists. There wasn't anything they could do about it since he is a geologist. Gregg dislikes him intensely. When I asked him why, he said that Alfred Shepley married his ex-wife, and that was evidence enough not to trust him."

"Why? Did he think Shepley might upset things at the dig?"

Frank frowned. "I'm not sure. Shepley certainly couldn't have stolen any fossils without the others knowing about it."

"Were there any open disagreements with Alfred Shepley?"

"None that I heard about. I wasn't up at the dig, however."

"How did Gregg act after Mary Jane arrived?"

Frank sighed. "He was angry about it. Mary Jane kept nagging him with caustic remarks about things that had happened during their marriage. Gregg tried to ignore her, but was furious most of the time. And then Mary Jane realized that Rhonda was in love with Gregg, and was trying to snare him. That made her furious."

"Gregg never met Rhonda anywhere? Did she sneak into his place at night?"

"No, I don't think so. Gregg is in love with Valerie Penrose, and Rhonda knew better than to try it without an invitation. Gregg would have thrown her out. He would have picked her up and thrown her into the dust in Frontier Street." He paused. "However, who knows what goes on in the dark around here? We all have to use outside plumbing, so no one questions anyone's nocturnal trips outside."

"Any ideas why Rhonda was killed? Or who did it?"

Again Frank frowned. "I think it has something to do with that pornography stuff. She was really after Gregg. He had a hell of a time trying to stay out of her way, but that doesn't mean he would try to kill her. After all, he was free to leave here at any time he wanted. Alfred could have taken over the recording of the strata at the site. But what if Rhonda really had taken pictures of them? Only I don't see how she could have rigged that up in this remote place. However, she slipped into my bed, so what about Mark and Derryck? And even Zach, although I think it would have made him puke."

"Is it possible, Frank, that she had something going with one of the scientists? There was a fossil bone found beside her body. She might have left it as a clue."

"I've never seen her with any of them, but who knows?"

"All right, let's forget that for now. Tell me about the evening Rhonda was killed. Where were you?"

Frank sighed. "That's just it. I was up on that old switchback on Mercury Mountain. It had been so hot that afternoon that I waited until evening to go up there. I returned to North Ledge just after dark. I wasn't with anyone, didn't see anyone. Gregg's place was dark, and I thought he was either in bed or still out at the swimming hole. So I didn't go over."

"Where was Rhonda during that last week? Did she stay here in North Ledge?"

"She stayed in North Ledge as far as I know, but I spend my days up on the mountains. There's no way of knowing what went on with these people at the hotel. Gregg probably knows more than I do because he sees Valerie whenever he has the chance. It took some doing for him to avoid both Mary Jane and Rhonda. You see, Rhonda thought she was irresistible, that Gregg wouldn't be able to resist her charms." He smiled in a wry way.

"And no one visited Rhonda?"

"There weren't many visitors. You can hear cars even up on the mountain. Besides, I think if there had been any, the artists would have mentioned it."

"Do you think Rhonda would have told any of the others about your relationship?" Deedra challenged.

"Who knows? She flaunted herself all the time. You know how those sexy gals in the movies do it. Well, she exaggerated even that. Derryck made fun of her all the time. He obviously loathed her."

Frank eyed the John Sinkankas book. "Is that Gregg's?"

"Yes. I needed a refresher about something I saw at Gregg's, some sketches that looked very familiar as if I'd seen something like it somewhere. Frank, I suppose anyone could have taken Gregg's knife since he was up at the dig most of the time. Do you take your knife with you?"

"Yes. I'm gone most of the time, some days I go into Grass Valley for supplies and to get in touch with the mining company. You know how long it takes over these roads. I'm gone most of the day then. I haven't used my knife in weeks, however."

"Do you take your mining notes with you when you leave North Ledge?"

"Yes, I take everything that can be used by the mining company, and I lock the other stuff in my 4-wheel rig."

"What about those young people? Does Gregg get along with them?"

"Yes. Rhonda was the only exception. No one got along with her. I think Gregg and Zach have a certain rapport. I know he doesn't really like Derryck…thinks he's got his gears meshed. Gregg's relationship with Shelley is strained because of their broken engagement.

I don't think he's made any special friends with any of them except Valerie."

"You mean Gregg was really engaged to Shelley Muldoon?" Deedra was totally surprised.

"Yeah. I don't know the details, only that they had a falling out when Shelley's parents wanted to interfere in Gregg's professional career. Wanted him to give it up and go into the family business. Gregg was on the rebound from his divorce and was vulnerable at the time, but he was never going to give up his career, and he wasn't deeply in love with Shelley either. Not like he is with Valerie."

"Frank, do you realize how mixed up all these relationships are? I had no idea Shelley was more than an acquaintance of Gregg's." She sighed. "However, that's no motive for Rhonda's murder. The motive for Rhonda's murder seems obscure, and I do think you're right in thinking it has something to do with Rhonda's writing which has its own dark side. That might or might not have given the other writers a strong motive.

"Rhonda was evidently up here to gather new material or hiding out from the vice squad." Deedra paused, thinking. "The thing about porn writers is that they have to keep thinking up more and more shocking things in order to sell their material. After a while, it just gets dull and they can't find a market. That keeps them looking for more and more lewd situations."

"I suppose so," Frank replied. "Just remember, I didn't kill Rhonda, but I'm not going to let Gregg get railroaded for it either."

In a glum mood, Frank went off toward his place. As Deedra watched him go, a jeans-clad figure skulked away from the scientists' living quarters, crossed over the Bridge Street Bridge and scurried down the creek.

She wasn't sure if Frank had seen Derryck Evans or not. She watched for several minutes, but did not see Derryck reappear.

She glanced up at the top floor of the old Frontier Hotel. Zach Johnson was standing at his window staring at the place where Derryck had vanished.

SIX

LATER THAT AFTERNOON, Deedra put on sturdy hiking gear, and headed up Jackson Creek to her destination, Mica Mountain. Not wanting to be seen, she forded the creek just beyond the bend where the creek meandered back toward Feather Mountain. Once on the far side of the mountain she left the cool shade along the creek and hiked toward the long abandoned mines. Here and there were rusting parts of mining equipment, boot soles curled with age, granite cooking utensils, and ancient barrel staves. The first of the old mines held nothing of interest either in its discarded tailings or the caved-in mine shafts. Only an experienced mining engineer like Frank would ever dare investigate such a mine.

Climbing at an angle was easier on the steep slope where its rubble gave way underfoot. She disturbed lizards and was on the watch for rattlesnakes. Deedra was deathly afraid of rattlesnakes; the hair on her neck tingled at the very thought of them.

The next series of mines produced nothing for either her mineral collection or offered any clues to Gregg's drawings. There was no telltale green of copper deposits in any of the rocks.

She climbed north toward a mine at the mountaintop. There she found several boulders with seams of dark green mixed with a rusty red color indicating a streak of iron. The green was of an opaque luster, rather greasy looking; characteristic of green jasper. It was not the trace of copper she was looking for, though all those rocks were merely surface float anyway. Still, if there was copper here, there should be evidences of it. The jasper only indicated silica, was a member of the quartz family of minerals. She couldn't shake the feeling that Gregg had found something important that he didn't want anyone to know about. Perhaps he was waiting to file a claim after the mixosaur dig was completed. The scientists, if they were aware of a valuable mineral deposit, would surely try to take advantage of it.

She walked back and forth, the thin air causing her to breathe heavily. She wondered if she was being observed by anyone in North Ledge. Gavin Blair didn't miss much that went on there. It gave her a sense of paranoia to think that even now, she might be observed through binoculars.

From the mountaintop she could see across North Ledge and the valleys on the far side of the North Ledge Range. Old mine tailings dotted the far side of Mica Mountain, and huddled in a narrow canyon was another ghost town whose buildings had suffered heavily from the ravages of time.

Deedra sat on the ridge memorizing the scene, the vision of the long-dead town where cool breezes riffled through trees and skittered down the slopes. Talus was scattered along the sides of the mountain.

Far off mountains were green with trees, but the mountains that surrounded North Ledge had only sparse, spindly trees, and young trees planted by a reforestation project. The area had been stripped barren by the necessities of life for the early frontier people. It was while she was studying the surroundings that she saw it, the clue to Gregg's drawings.

She had turned to look north and caught a glassy shimmer out of the corner of her eye. She glanced back toward North Ledge. No movement there seemed to have caused it. When she slowly turned again, the shining glitter shone from a place where the earth had recently been disturbed. It was a small translucent gem in hexagonal crystal form of a faint greenish-color. A beryl crystal. It lacked the blue of the aquamarine and the green of the emerald. Nevertheless, it was a true gemstone.

Excitement rushed through her. She carefully examined the topsoil knowing that if she hadn't seen the crystal, she wouldn't have noticed that the earth had been disturbed there.

The mines were not as high on the slope as those on the North Ledge side. Then she noted a boulder that had been moved several inches to the left. With her miner's pick she dug at its base and opened up a cavity, a vug. Large crystals of quartz lined the top side, though a few loose crystals lay on top of the colorful mineral lining. The flashlight illuminated large beryl crystals "in situ" crosswise of the vug. They were the sea-green color of gem aquamarines. If, she mused, there was this vug then there would be others deeper in the mountain. It was a rich find. No wonder Gregg remained silent about it.

Deedra stood up, glanced over the ridge into North Ledge. Though there was no visible movement, someone could still be watching her. After taking several loose crystals, she pushed the dirt and rocks back over the vug.

Even though Gregg didn't want anyone to know about his find, she didn't think it had anything to do with Rhonda Adams' murder.

Gregg had sketched the vug not only because of its geologic importance, but because of its value. Perhaps Gregg had thought the scientists might try to take it over. It was more likely that he didn't want any publicity about it. News about a discovery like that would bring the amateurs out like fleas, and the mountains would be littered with diggers and claim jumpers.

She hiked along the far slope hoping she couldn't be seen from North Ledge. She constantly varied her path so that if anyone was watching her, it would be harder to tell if she had found anything or where she'd been. She traveled north, crossing the draw where Mica Mountain and Feather Mountain joined, where native vegetation struggled for life between boulders of mica, gneiss, and mixed porphyry. These boulders were rounded, telling of time in ancient waters. Others with rough jagged edges had broken off the surrounding cliffs.

A path through the draw showed signs of recent travel. At several places boulders and smaller rocks had been splintered by miner's picks. Frank Shundo had probably searched there, though any of the scientists and roaming rock-hounds might have left those marks. There was no trace of copper-green. Mesquite covered the slope and had turned the dull color of mid-summer. The path wandered into North Ledge Valley. She was still too far away to see it, however. Only the trees along Jackson Creek were visible. She had walked further than she had intended.

She crossed Jackson Creek on large boulders near the

vehicle ford, then quickly climbed to the old stage road, avoiding places where rattlesnakes slithered between rocks and brush.

It was hot. Deedra was anxious to get back to the cool shade along Jackson Creek where it flowed beside North Ledge. Her footsteps blended with the buzz of insects and the occasional slithering as lizards raced for cover.

As she had suspected, Gavin was seated beside Jackson Creek his binoculars trained on Mica Mountain. Quietly she approached the bridge. The sheriff was aware of her footsteps before he realized she was almost at his side.

GAVIN COULDN'T CONTROL his surprise.

Deedra laughed to herself knowing she had outwitted the sheriff. At the same time she was rueful at knowing that her actions had been under surveillance. She turned and went back to the old church.

She wanted to hide the crystals, but didn't want to disturb the old planking of the church knowing that it would attract attention if anyone searched. In the dim light that filtered through the high windows, she studied the gems. There were the pink and green ones of tourmaline, the mineral with the piezieolectricity characteristics; positive on one end, negative on the other. Those positive and negative characteristics made them valuable for industrial purposes as well as their gemstone quality for jewelry. The beryl crystal was a glowing aquamarine of value, with good color and no fractures. She left the quartz crystal in her pack and put the gem crystals in her jeans pocket, not knowing where to hide them.

At least now she knew the reason for Gregg's aura of secrecy, for his uneasiness, his reluctance to talk about the sketches. She debated whether to tell Gavin, and finally decided against it. It really wasn't her secret, and it would only create additional problems for Gregg and also the murder investigation. Unless Rhonda had discovered the deposit, or wanted a share of it, she didn't think it had anything to do with the murder.

Deedra was brought abruptly back to reality by the sound of heavy footsteps outside the church. A stab of fear shot through her.

"Who's there?"

"It's me, Brent. Where the heck have you been?"

Relief flooded through her. "Up on Mica Mountain. You should have asked Gavin, he's been watching through the binoculars!" Deedra laughed, held the door open.

"Find anything up there?"

"Um," Deedra muttered. "Have you got photos of everyone?"

Brent nodded, still waiting for her to tell him why she had climbed Mica Mountain. When Deedra didn't volunteer, Brent shrugged, dismissing it as trivial.

Deedra told Brent about Frank's visit, his claim of innocence, even though he and Rhonda had a secret affair. That he was afraid that Gavin would learn of it, and that if Gregg was charged with Rhonda's murder, he would then tell Gavin to diminish the suspicion against Gregg.

"I don't blame him for not wanting that to be known," Brent agreed. "You know how the scandal sheets would take off on that!" He sighed. "What's the most damaging for Gregg is that knife. Of course, you could also say that no one knew where Frank was. His statement of being up on Mercury Mountain can't be proved. And right now, with his own confession, he has a stronger motive than Gregg. But the very fact that both Gregg and Frank knew Rhonda before arriving at North Ledge is damaging."

Deedra nodded glumly. "What have those young people been doing this afternoon?" Deedra was trying to keep her mind off how excited she was over the discovery of the gem deposit.

Brent ran a hand through his thick tangle of hair. "They all went down to the creek in back of the scientists' quarters. There's a clearing there where they work on hot days. It really gets muggy in those old buildings. They work without saying a word to each other, it's spooky it's so quiet. Guess that's what you call concentration. Sure is different in a newspaper office."

Deedra walked to the door, looked toward the place Brent had told her about. She noted that Mica Mountain couldn't be observed by the young people from there. The store building blocked the view. She breathed a sigh of relief.

Brent walked up behind her, cupped her breasts with his hands, and kissed her ear. "Do you know that I really love you? Shall we run off to Vegas and get married? Leave this murder case to the professionals? Would you resent missing that front page byline?"

He paused when he saw the flicker of doubt in her eyes. "I know, it would make you miserable and me feel guilty, and I do have a commitment to my paper. We'll just have to postpone things a bit longer."

So once again Deedra's love life was put on hold, but they pledged eternal love.

Between kisses they discussed the murder, how they would write the stories, which suspect had the strongest motive. They finally agreed that Mary Jane had the strongest motive, and could have killed Rhonda in a fit of jealousy. How they could prove that was probably going to be difficult.

"Frank swears he didn't kill Rhonda, and didn't set Gregg up. He reminded me of how close he and Gregg were in those early years, and unless Frank Shundo has changed in the last few years, he wouldn't have killed Rhonda to make Gregg look guilty."

"Don't lose your perspective, Deedra. People are changed by circumstances, and we don't know what happened during those years, and the weeks preceding the murder."

"Um," Deedra replied. She knew that Brent's reasoning was sound, but she could not bring herself to believe that either Frank or Gregg had committed murder. And even though tempted, she didn't confide about her discovery of the gem deposit, and that she believed it was Gregg's secret. It was a temptation to show him the gemstones, but she recalled that Brent had always regarded her rock collecting with sly amusement as if she had to be indulged for some eccentric activity. Now that she had found something really valuable it was difficult not to show them to him with an "I told you so."

SEVEN

DEEDRA WAS NEVER to forget that evening, one of the most frightening she had ever lived through.

Deedra, Brent, and Gavin suppered along the banks of Jackson Creek where the moving water gave off a semblance of coolness. Gavin told them the history of North Ledge, how an old miner had been grubstaked by a friend. How he had set out with a pack burro from North San Juan eventually striking it rich at North Ledge. Ledge Michaels, the miner, had camped practically where they sat along Jackson Creek, had panned gold from the creek itself. He had followed the creek up to Quartz Mountain, had located the first mine in that area naming it the Golden Ledge. It had started a rush, though North Ledge had never reached the grandeur of other boomtowns, even though the gold veins were richer, but the veins shallow and were soon worked out.

Gavin told them of the hanging in North Ledge when a claim jumper had killed Ledge Michaels, and tried to take over the Golden Ledge mine. There had been a squabble over it, resulting in the death of one miner and the wounding of several others. A miner named Black Jack Kelly had finally taken over the claim by force. He had to guard it constantly. One day he vanished. Later his body was found on Mercury Mountain too decomposed to discover the cause of death.

"When the gold ledge ran out at the turn of the century, everyone left North Ledge, but an old prospector who set up his home in the Wells Fargo station, and continued to look for the elusive bonanza. He died during the winter of 1929. North Ledge was abandoned except for sporadic visits by rock-hounds and geologists. Not until Frank Shundo arrived, had anyone really lived in North Ledge."

When darkness brought out a host of bugs and strange crawly things, they drifted back to North Ledge where they stood outside Gavin's office talking in low tones, exchanging tales of news reporting and law enforcement. There was movement now and then at the hotel. Frank arrived from the direction of Mercury Mountain, went into his place and then out again. They could hear the young people laughing while they swam and splashed in Jackson Creek. There was no sign of Gregg, and Deedra surmised that he was swimming with the others. A light shone from the scientists' quarters.

Deedra said goodnight to the men and started toward the old church when Mary Jane's scream echoed about the old ghost town in haunting refrain.

For an instant Deedra thought time stood still.

Then she saw Gavin and Brent run toward Dead Man's Alley. She raced after them.

Mary Jane's flashlight beam outlined Alfred Shepley's body, a knife protruding from his back. He was obviously dead, his life's blood spreading into the dust of Dead Man's Alley.

The screams attracted everyone. Deedra carefully

noted from which direction they arrived. All the young people and Gregg ran up Dead Man's Alley from the swimming hole on the other side of the blacksmith's shop. Even Derryck Evans. The scientists and Frank arrived together from the other direction.

Brent nudged Deedra. "Knife is just like the one that killed Rhonda."

Except that this knife had a deep scratch on the hilt, but no initials.

In the light from Gavin's strong flashlight Deedra saw Frank stare at the knife in an almost hypnotic state, his face pale and pinched. She guessed then that the knife was his.

Gavin ordered Brent to turn on his 4-wheel rig lights so that the alley was better illuminated. Brent's rig was parked in front of his place at the end of the alley facing Frontier Street. When the lights flashed on Deedra was still studying Frank, and he must have felt her scrutiny for he looked at her with a helpless, hopeless look that disturbed the usual tranquility of his eyes, and pulled down the corners of his mouth.

Deedra shook her head slightly, cautioning Frank to keep quiet.

Gavin shook Mary Jane to stop her half-hearted screams, than asked, "What happened?"

Mary Jane appeared to pull herself together, though Deedra had the feeling that she was putting on an act—that she was aware of everything that went on around her. That her grief for Alfred was just a surface thing.

"Alfred went out to get some air. The young people were making so much noise we couldn't go to sleep. When he didn't return I went looking for him. I stumbled over him!"

Deedra and Brent exchanged glances in sudden alertness. Mary Jane's story was all too smooth, like it had been rehearsed. They had both seen relatives of victims in first shock, and knew they sounded disjointed, upset, often leaving sentences hanging in midair. Mary Jane did not act shocked like others they had seen. Had she killed her husband?

Gavin examined the body. "Been dead for an hour or so looks like," he muttered. "How long did you say he'd been gone before you started looking for him?"

"I don't know, an hour perhaps," Mary Jane replied.

Gavin gave Brent and Deedra a look indicating disgust which Deedra interpreted as "no way to find out who killed him."

Deedra wondered why she and Brent hadn't noticed Alfred slip out of his saloon home, then realized he had probably gone out the back door. His body lay in the dust several feet beyond Brent's abode, as if he had been returning from the blacksmith's shop. She was certain that their conversation couldn't have been overheard in the alley, and Alfred might not have even been aware of their presence there. However, sound did carry in that old ghost town. The more likely event was that someone had hidden in the shadows and waited for Alfred to pass by. It did not appear to be a random killing.

The sheriff's thoughts must have been similar for she saw him glance from the alley to his office, then along the side of Brent's place. From where they had been standing, they wouldn't have been able to observe any movement in the alley. It was an eerie feeling to know that they had stood only a few yards away while the killer went about his round of death. They hadn't even been aware that anyone was in the alley, the night was that dark. The moon hadn't yet peered over North Ledge Range. The buildings were simply dark silhouettes in a murky night. The killer had utilized the darkness, made it part of his modus operandi.

"Where have you all been this evening?" Gavin began his interrogation.

The young people looked at each other, seeking support. Again only Frank had been out in the dark alone. He had gone to the creek at a place just beyond the swimming hole to wash up. She knew Frank had returned from his trek up the mountain, and then had gone out again. They had presumed he had gone to wash up. But it was Frank's knife that had been the murder weapon this time.

She shuddered.

Only Mary Jane had known that Alfred was in Dead Man's Alley. Gregg and Valerie had been up near Boothill Ridge evidently in a lovemaking mood. The others all claimed to have been at the swimming hole, the scientists claimed to have been in their rooms having retired early.

Derryck remarked, "If you didn't see anything, Sheriff, and you were standing right there in front of your office, why do you expect that any of us saw anything? It's hellishly dark tonight. Anyone could have sneaked up on sneaky old Al!"

Derryck stated what they had all been thinking. Deedra didn't miss his reference to "sneaky" Alfred. What had given Derryck that impression?

Brent took photos. After Gavin questioned everyone he sent them to their quarters, making notations in an official looking notebook. "You two," Gavin said to Brent and Deedra, "stay right there. I don't want anyone destroying the evidence. I've got to call the D.A."

Brent and Deedra could hear him calling on his police radio. The sound of his voice floated on the silent night air, a harsh reminder that civilization lurked just beyond the mountains.

"Deedra, hold this camera. I want to see what's in Alfred's pockets." Carefully Brent went through the dead man's pockets, finding only a penknife and change. In his wallet was money, lots of money, though Brent didn't count it. It ruled out the possibility that he had been robbed. Pictures of Mary Jane, his I.D., driver's license, and credit cards. Nothing unusual.

"Can't tell anything from the footprints around here either," Deedra remarked. "Where did Mary Jane go?"

"To her house. Derryck is with her." Brent gave Deedra a questioning glance.

Gavin returned. "The District Attorney's arranged for the removal of the body. He's on his way up here with the police photographers. Hope you took pictures, Brent. I need some of my own to work with, and once the D.A. gets his hands on evidence, I don't really get a good look at it."

Brent and Deedra chuckled. Both had met the politician-type in their newspaper work.

"Don't get me wrong. The D.A. does a super job, just pompous as hell, and thinks I don't know anything."

Again they laughed. It wasn't what Gavin said, but the tone of disgust in his voice that amused them.

Gavin searched Alfred's body in much the same manner as Brent had only a few minutes earlier. Gavin counted the money, and carefully noted the amount in his notebook. He had several hundred dollars on him.

"You two had better get some rest. After the D.A. gets here, none of us will get any sleep."

"Want me to walk you up to the church, Deedra?" Brent asked.

Deedra knew that Brent wanted to stay around Gavin, so replied, "No, I'm not afraid of the dark."

Gavin gave her an uneasy glance. "I don't think Alfred was either."

Deedra wasn't as brave as she wanted the men to think, and the echoes of her footsteps resounded as she crossed the old bridge, setting her teeth on edge as the sound reverberated into the dark places. She tried to silence the sound of her footfalls, not wanting anyone to know she was alone. Even in the dark the killer would know that only one person crossed that bridge. A shiver or premonition shook her. She glanced into each shadow alongside the road. Those murky shadows were threatening, like they might hold unknown terrors. The way to the church seemed longer in the darkness, and she wondered why she didn't insist on quarters closer to the others. Perhaps it would be wise to move into the old hotel.

Finally, Deedra left the dirt road and climbed the knoll to the church, glancing up at the roof where the cross was silhouetted against the night sky.

She didn't hear the sound behind her. It was only the fact that she turned her ankle on a rock and lurched off to the right that saved her life. The killer's knife struck her in the upper arm. It felled her instantly.

She sank to the ground unconscious, unaware that the

killer searched her, and when he found the gems muttered, "Ah."

Deedra was left for dead in the shadow of the old Catholic church, the wound oozing around the knife buried in her upper arm. The killer heard a noise that forced him to leave before he could make certain that she was dead.

The night cooled. After a time the night creatures resumed their prowling, sometimes pausing to sniff and stare at the unconscious news reporter.

In North Ledge, Gavin Blair stood guard over Alfred Shepley's body hoping that nothing else would happen before he caught the killer, and wondering how long it would take the District Attorney to arrive. He didn't relish another visit, knowing that they would wonder why he hadn't seen or heard the killer.

EIGHT

THE SOUND OF police sirens woke Deedra. When she opened her eyes, the reptilian orbs of a ring-necked lizard were watching her with ancient curiosity, ready to scurry away at the slightest threat.

It was early morning, though the sun hadn't yet climbed over North Ledge Range. The night chill had receded, leaving her joints stiff. A sharp pain in her shoulder accompanied her movements. She groaned.

The lizard scurried off with a scaly, slithery sound.

Blood had stiffened her blouse. She couldn't keep from groaning when she tried to get up. Until that movement the sprained ankle hadn't been the source of the most pain. Black spots flashed across her vision and nausea shook her. She grabbed a mesquite branch and clung to it until the dizziness passed.

The siren noise grew louder. The engine sounds told her several vehicles were approaching.

She limped into the church knowing she couldn't walk into North Ledge until she had bandaged her ankle and gotten something around the knife wound.

The church door opened with a screech, protesting loudly in the morning air. She hoped the killer wasn't around listening for sounds that would tell him she was still alive.

Leaning against the wall for support, she rummaged about in the pack for the first aid kit. Holding a navy blue bandanna in her right hand to preserve any fingerprints on the knife, she withdrew it from the wound. Pain shot through her. She muffled the screams between clenched teeth, quickly placed a pressure bandage over the wound, and pressed her arm against the wall to stop the bleeding, thus creating another pressure bandage.

After a moment or two of fighting dizziness, she opened a vial of ammonia. With a whiff, the black spots vanished. Gradually the pain receded and the fresh bleeding stopped.

She stripped off her blouse, covered the wound with triangular bandages and strips of surgical tape. She put on a man's shirt, and tied a sling around her arm using her teeth. There was a stretch bandage in the first aid kit that she tied around her ankle. It did not occur to her to look for the gems she had previously stashed in her jeans pocket.

After eating a few crackers and washing them down with bottled water, she limped toward Gavin's office. Even in last night's darkness the trek had not seemed that long. The rough road caused ankle pain. Twice she was forced to stop until the pain faded away.

When finally she reached the bridge, Brent saw her, and began running toward her. Gavin followed with a long ambling lope. This attracted the attention of a uniformed officer who began to run after them. Brent was first to reach her side, his camera flopping. The morning light outlined the sudden anxiety on his face.

"I didn't want the whole damn police force," Deedra muttered as Gavin and the policeman galloped up.

"Deedra!" Brent had a dazed expression, then without waiting for an explanation, picked her up, and carried her to the police ambulance. Fortunately, they hadn't yet loaded Alfred's body, and the police surgeon was able to perform his medical arts in a sterile surrounding.

"What happened?" the doctor asked in a sympathetic tone.

"I was stabbed last night. I turned my ankle and that's what saved me."

The doctor informed the hovering Gavin that he could question her after she received the proper medical attention.

The District Attorney saw the commotion around the ambulance and hurried up in time to overhear the conversation.

Deedra saw that everyone had gathered on Frontier Street. There was a hushed silence as if no one dared breathe loudly. The scene was forever imprinted on her mind.

Doctor John Brendan quickly and efficiently tended her wounds, gave her a shot of antibiotic, and a bottle of pain pills from his medical bag. "You did a neat job bandaging that wound. Do you have first aid training?"

"Yes. My job can be dangerous at times," she laughed in a brittle way.

The doctor gave her a clinical look, noting her eyes and pallor, and frowned.

Deedra was impatient, anxious to know what was going on, needing to get the story, wanting to meet the District Attorney. Gavin's description caused her curiosity.

Dr. Brendan cautioned, "Ah, ah, ah! Let's not get excited now. Let that other newsman get the information. You need rest. A night on the ground didn't cure that shock, you know."

Deedra didn't answer, listening to the strange voices, not able to hear what was said. Her news reporter instinct struggled at the delay. She was more concerned with the story than with her health right now.

When Dr. Brendan finished doctoring, Deedra felt more like herself. He felt she didn't need a sling. After thanking him she stepped from the ambulance into the incredible scene in Dead Man's Alley.

ALFRED SHEPLEY'S BODY still lay sprawled in the dust. Uniformed officers stood about taking depositions, a paunchy man with a bald head minced about talking first to one person, and then another. Gavin stood off to one side with Brent and watched, letting the District Attorney take over the investigation. His name was Marlin Narkette and he was deceptively obtuse. Under that bald pate was a shrewd, calculating mind devoted to keeping himself in office.

Deedra studied Narkette. He was undoubtedly brilliant. The problem was he didn't think anyone else was intelligent. He treated the officers as if they were flunkies. He was, however, not a person Deedra would care to cross. She suspected that he was an honest, ambitious man. But he reminded her of men who though honest themselves, overlooked graft and fraud in others if it furthered their political careers. Deedra had met his type before. She knew that whoever was arrested for the murders of Rhonda Adams and Alfred Shepley would undoubtedly be convicted based on this man's determination. Fear for Gregg and Frank caused her mouth to dry with anxiety.

When the D.A. saw Deedra standing beside the ambulance, he sent everyone back to their abodes with instructions to remain there for the time being.

Narkette gestured Deedra into Gavin's office where she could sit in Gavin's chair. Gavin, Brent, and the doctor arranged themselves about the room as if to protect her from some terrible fate.

Narkette asked, "Miss Masefield, take your time and tell me exactly where you were and when you were stabbed."

After Deedra related the happenings, the D.A. sent an officer to the church to retrieve her blouse and the knife.

"You didn't see anyone or hear anyone? Smell anything like cigarette smoke or perfumes like those used in colognes or soaps?"

"No. There wasn't any sound or any other indication that anyone was around. I was unsettled, of course, nervous. We had just discovered Alfred's body and the walk to the old church in the dark was scary. So I was listening for sounds."

The D.A. turned to Gavin. "Where was everyone?"

"I'd sent them all back to their quarters. Brent was with me. I didn't see anyone leave their place, though it was easy enough to have done that without being seen from Dead Man's Alley. I couldn't see the church from there."

The D.A. took a turn around the room scratching his bald pate. "That means it could have been anyone. With no inside plumbing here, everyone is outside at some time or other at night."

Gavin nodded. "That's just it. There's really no way to prove just where everyone was. The church can be reached by numerous ways. It's easy to get there without even walking on the old stage road. That's why Rhonda's murder isn't all cut and dried. Anyone could have killed her. None of the residents here really has an airtight alibi. It's only the fact that Gregg's initials were scratched into the knife handle that causes us to suspect him."

Just then the officer returned. "The knife isn't there. I searched everywhere."

"What?" Deedra distinctly remembered laying the knife on the floor.

The police officer shook his head.

Narkette looked at the police surgeon. "She couldn't have stabbed herself?"

The doctor shook his head.

Brent, his hair still messed as if he had forgotten to comb it, asked, "Deedra, was the knife like the others?"

"Yes. It was similar to the one that was used to stab Alfred."

The D.A. ordered the officers to go out and attempt to round up all the knives in North Ledge. Deedra knew the D.A. would be searching for signs of human blood on them. Only Gregg's knife should be missing.

"Miss Masefield, why are you dangerous to the killer? What is it that you have discovered?"

Deedra shook her head. "I don't know." Though she thought the killer had probably seen her caution Frank not to say it was his knife sticking in Shepley's back. Only she knew that Frank's knife had a deep scratch in it. With the information that Frank had told her, the District Attorney might make a very tight case. Not wanting to give the D.A. that information caused her to restrict her comments.

"There had to be an obvious motive for the attack on

you. Are you sure you don't have evidence of some kind, or maybe saw something that would give you a clue to the killer?" Narkette was like a bloodhound on the scent.

Suddenly she recalled the gems, touched her jeans pocket, and realized for the first time that the crystals were gone. That meant the killer had searched her. The thought angered her. How dare he touch her? But how did the crystals have anything to do with Rhonda's murder, or Alfred Shepley's?

Brent glanced at her.

She sent him a long look that warned him not to question, to change the subject.

Gavin's eyes suddenly narrowed. He was thinking back to the discovery of Alfred's body, and what had happened in those few minutes following that discovery. Remembering that Brent and Deedra had been left alone while he called in on the police radio. Deedra could almost hear his thoughts.

"Did you see anything suspicious last night, Deedra? See anyone while we were standing in front of my office?" Gavin's eyes were like steely points of inquisition.

She shook her head. She was trying to remember who might have seen her send that warning look at Frank not to tell that the murder knife was his. Who had been watching? Derryck, Steven Robbins, Shelley, and perhaps Dr. Kurt Von Kraus. If she recalled correctly, the others had been staring at Mary Jane or at Alfred's body. Even that wasn't certain; the scene had only been illuminated by emergency lights.

"You're certain you didn't even hint that you knew something about the killer?" The D.A wasn't about to drop the subject.

"Frank Shundo came to see me yesterday, someone could have seen Frank go into the church, and might have listened to what he had to tell me. That's the only unusual thing that's happened until I was stabbed."

"And was that conversation with Frank damaging to Alfred or the killer?"

"No. It was only something personal. Frank and I have known each other since our teen years. It was just a talk." She sighed. "I think Alfred was killed because he saw the killer in the alley either before Rhonda was murdered or afterwards."

Narkette looked as if he had discovered the clue which would solve the murders.

Deedra glanced at Brent and saw the flicker of warning in his eyes.

Her statement, however, had distracted the District Attorney. He was jotting a notation in his notebook. She supposed it was a reminder to question Frank.

"Now, I need to question Gregg Dancer."

The police sergeant cautioned, "Do you suppose you should? Dancer doesn't have an attorney, and if you arrest him later he can claim you didn't read him his rights, that he didn't have a chance to get an attorney to represent him. That one wasn't available up here."

"I'll ask him if he has any objection, and read him his rights," Narkette replied. "He can object if he wants to." The District Attorney knew that Gregg wouldn't object—knew he needed to cooperate with the law.

Deedra glanced at Gavin, giving him a silent salute. Gavin had indeed judged the D.A. correctly. Narkette underestimated the sheriff's intelligence and his knowledge of human nature. The sheriff had no illusions about life. He was also Gregg's ally, and if Gregg was to be exonerated, it would take all of Gavin's, Brent's and her own efforts.

THE OFFICERS SENT to round up the knives returned with further mysterious news. Only Mary Jane's and Valerie's knives had been found. The others had suddenly disappeared.

"When did you last see those knives?" Narkette whirled on Gavin.

"Right after Rhonda Adams' murder."

"Were they all here then? Who owned knives like that?"

"All the men owned knives and said so. The women didn't admit they owned any. Gregg Dancer's was the only one missing."

"The women said they didn't own any?"

"That's right. I suspected they had them for protection though. No one really goes to a remote place like this without some sort of weapon. Especially women."

The D.A. nodded. "Strange." He turned to the officers. "Search the empty buildings. See if you can find those knives stashed away somewhere."

The men went out and Brent followed. The empty buildings were the blacksmith shop, the old livery stable, and the ramshackle house remains just beyond the church.

Again Marlin Narkette had Deedra go over the events just before her attack. When she finished reciting the events he asked the police surgeon, "How serious is that wound?"

"Superficial. In the muscle, but no ligaments were cut. It's just going to be painful with no permanent damage. Deedra's suffering more from shock and exposure. After all, she was out on the ground all night with that wound and got thoroughly chilled."

"Couldn't have stabbed herself, right?" He asked again, and not wanting Dr. Brendan to respond, "Say, aren't you Deedra Masefield, the investigative reporter for the *Daily Spokesman?* You solved that crazy case up in Bermondy." The D.A.'s eyes widened with sudden wariness.

Deedra nodded, noting the police sergeant start. It was a sudden almost imperceptible movement. Deedra knew the news had taken him by surprise. The sergeant realized that he should have recognized her immediately.

There was a moment of stunned silence abruptly punctuated by shouts from the direction of the livery stable. Then another silence, then the sound of running footsteps along the alley. Everyone in the room tensed, their eyes turned toward the open door.

The officers and Brent stepped inside the room. One of the officers was carrying something in a large bandanna. He laid it on Gavin's makeshift desk, then carefully unfolded it revealing a clutter of knives. All were hunting knives, and all were very similar to the murder weapons.

He looked at the D.A. "They were in the far corner of that old livery stable. They could have been dropped there from outside the building. There's a plank missing in the wall. The killer probably dropped them there while walking along Jackson Creek."

NINE

No one moved. The knives shimmered in the dim light. Everyone looked at them with evil fascination. Brent took pictures. Deedra wondered if the killer had placed the knives there. Or maybe Frank had done it to keep them from discovering that his knife was missing. She sighed.

The discovery, however, caused everyone to relax.

The fingerprint technician took over and dusted each knife for prints. Everyone watched closely as the tech did his work. Brent took photos of the process, earning the ire of the police photographer who thought Brent was stealing his thunder. There were eight knives and every knife had been wiped clean. There were no identifying marks on them, no way of telling who owned them. Only Mary Jane and Valerie still had their knives.

The District Attorney realized the impossibility of trying to identify the knives. Though they weren't actual evidence, he confiscated them to prevent further "accidents."

"I'm going to question everyone again. Then we might as well go back to the city. Not much else I can do up here. I'm going to leave a man here, Blair. Send him out with any physical evidence or reports you need to get to me. Just continue with the investigation. I have the feeling that Gregg Dancer didn't do it. There's something cockeyed about the evidence. You don't kill someone with a knife that has your own initials on it and then leave it at the scene. Just doesn't add up somehow." Narkette was still muttering to himself as he went toward the scientists' living quarters.

Brent trailed after the D.A. Deedra wanted to, though the disapproving eye of the police surgeon kept her in Gavin's rickety old chair. The chair was wired together with baling wire that Gavin had found in the old ghost town, but was nevertheless, the only comfortable chair in town.

Gavin glanced at Deedra whose sea-blue eyes were clouded with pain and shock. Deedra felt his scrutiny and knew that he, too, was wondering what she knew and what she had discovered. Deedra wasn't yet ready to tell them; instinctively knowing that somehow the knowledge could help trap the killer. She had already half-formed a plan. It would take a day or two to put into action. She had to give herself time to get over the effects of the assault. She was beginning to think Rhonda's murder had been a mistake...that the victim was supposed to have been Gregg.

"I saw you climb Mica Mountain yesterday, Deedra. Did you find anything interesting up there?" Gavin's tone was casual, though she sensed his underlying motive.

"There's another ghost town on the other side of the mountain and another creek, though I didn't see any road leading into it."

"There isn't a road now. Years ago a landslide cut off the town, though it was already a ghost town by then. It's named Crucible. The people there climbed over the mountain to attend church in North Ledge. It was the only church around these parts." Gavin paused, shifted his weight on the other leg and resumed. "The road from Crucible cut through a draw, then down the old stage road to North Ledge. From there they could get out to the larger towns. You ought to get Brent to take photos of that old town before you leave. Another few years and it will be completely destroyed."

"Any of the people here been interested in it?"

Gavin looked surprised as if something had just occurred to him. "I don't know. I suppose they've all gone over there."

"Could Rhonda have had a rendezvous with someone over there?"

"Perhaps. How about you and me and Brent riding over? We can get across that draw in one of the 4-wheel rigs."

Deedra's eyes sparkled with the prospect of exploring the old place. They planned the trip for the next day, barring any complications.

"I certainly hope there won't be another attempt on your life," Gavin frowned. "I don't like you up there at the old church all alone."

"Don't worry, Gavin. I'm not afraid, and once I'm inside I'll be okay."

Gavin shook his head, not at all convinced that Deedra was safe from another attack. "Maybe you should move into one of the vacant rooms in the old hotel."

"Stop worrying, Gavin. You asked me up here for a purpose, remember?"

Dr. John Brendan went to supervise the removal of Alfred Shepley's body. Deedra hurried to watch, glad to get away from Gavin's worried looks.

It was a grisly sight, the lifting of the dead man out of the dust and dirt of Dead Man's Alley. Deedra noticed that rigor mortis had set in.

Mary Jane Shepley stood in front of the saloon home where she and Alfred had lived during their stay in North Ledge. Deedra wondered if Mary Jane planned to stay there now that Alfred's needs were no more. Strange that both the men she had married ended up here.

Suspicion of the woman caused Deedra to recall what she knew about Mary Jane: a selfish, grasping woman, never really happy, not certain that any man was good enough for her. What was it with her, what did she really want out of life? If she had expected sympathy from Gregg, she must have been disappointed. Gregg was staying away, not even mingling with the other young people. Deedra knew that being suspected of murder had upset him.

The D.A. had finished questioning Dr. Robbins, Dr. Von Kraus, and Dr. Drake, because Deedra saw him at the window of Zach's studio on the top floor of the old hotel. She giggled to herself thinking of Narkette's reaction to Derryck's and Rhonda's studios.

"Gavin, did any of those young people give you any idea about Rhonda's activities? Were they chummy with Alfred?"

"Rhonda was jealous of Gregg's visiting Valerie Penrose and was glad when the Shepleys arrived, which put a stop to Gregg's visiting Valerie at the old hotel. Valerie told me that she and Gregg talked a lot about art. Surprisingly, Gregg was drawing some sketches of the mountains and buildings around here.

From what Valerie told me, she obviously hated and feared Rhonda, who made scathing remarks about her."

"Sketches? Have you seen them?"

"No. I never asked Gregg about them. Do you think they have anything to do with Rhonda's murder?"

"Gregg is very artistic, Gavin. He often sketched things when he was young. I'm sure he never abandoned the habit. It would be interesting to know if he sketched Rhonda or Rhonda with someone."

Gavin paced up and down in front of the alley. He was obviously waiting for the return of the D.A. The lab men had finished their routine work in Dead Man's Alley and returned to their police van. "I'm more interested in Gregg's talks with Rhonda. I'm certain they talked or met somewhere around here. Rhonda had to base her love for Gregg on more than just seeing him from a distance."

Deedra frowned. Gavin was right. Had Gregg met Rhonda secretly after they moved up here? Had Valerie learned of it? Perhaps Rhonda threatened to break up Valerie and Gregg as she had done with Gregg and Shelley. Deedra was hampered by not knowing about Gregg's life since he went to college. Still, she didn't believe he had killed them, even though he acted distant, not friendly and trusting like Frank Shundo. Did Frank suspect that Gregg had killed Rhonda? Was that his reason for trying to steer Deedra's attention away from Gregg?

She leaned against the old hitching rail where she could watch everything except the scientists' quarters. That was the thing that bothered her most. The three scientists were able to leave and return to their living quarters without being seen by anyone. If they left by way of the front door, they could be seen by Zach and Rhonda from their upstairs studios, but when they were working they may not have noticed anything. And Zach couldn't see the Shepleys place from his studio.

District Attorney Narkette walked out of the Frontier Hotel. Instead of going to the center of the street, he kept to the shade of sparse trees growing between the hotel and Frank's place. Deedra thought he must be on his way to see Frank.

He suddenly cursed, noticed something in the dirt, and shouted. He pushed at the dirt with the toe of his shoe.

"Here it is!" Narkette shouted to Gavin.

Narkette took an immaculate white handkerchief from his pocket and reached down into the dust where he picked up another hunting knife. Without a doubt it was the knife used to stab Deedra. There were still dark stains on the blade.

TEN

THE KNIFE CAUGHT a ray of sunlight and glittered. The tech quickly took it to the police van where it could be examined with their portable equipment. Dr. Brendan took a sample of Deedra's blood for spectroscopic examination to see if it matched that on the knife blade, though they were all certain that it would.

Luckily Brent had been on the scene, and took photos of the D.A. finding the knife, a real scoop for him and his newspaper.

There were no telltale fingerprints on the knife and no footprints in the dust. The dust was inches deep and any prints there had been stirred up by Narkette himself. It hadn't rained in months. The killer could have thrown the knife there from across the street, from the hotel, from the scientists' quarters, or from Frank's and Gregg's places. The killer wouldn't even have had to walk to where it was found.

The D.A. was jubilant at having found the missing knife.

Deedra laughed to herself wondering how the District Attorney planned to cross-examine himself about the discovery of the knife. She didn't, however, put those thoughts into words. To make an enemy of Narkette might put the *Daily Spokesman* under suspicion and harassment.

Narkette urged everyone into the police vehicles without interrogating Frank. Perhaps the discovery of the knife had changed his mind. Regardless, the rest of the group watched the law entourage drive off toward North San Juan with obvious relief.

Gavin and Brent walked Deedra to a cool place along Jackson Creek where they ordered her to rest, and not to move from there without letting them know where she went. They then returned to Gavin's office for a man-to-man conference.

As Deedra watched the water bubble and gurgle over the rounded rocks, cleansing and cooling the creek bed, she relived the preceding evening when the killer had struck without warning. Again she searched her memory for a clue. There had been no warning noise, only that strange premonition as she walked across the bridge and up that lonely road. Would the one who had waited there in the shadows try again? A shudder skimmed along her spine.

Deedra's eyes closed. She slept. Most of the residents of the old ghost town saw her sleeping there and went to a clearing along the creek on the other side of Bridge Street to avoid waking her.

The silence in North Ledge was broken only by the buzzing of gnats and dragonflies, and the weird slithering of crawly creatures moving in the sagebrush and under the shale rocks.

Brent had called both newspapers right after the D.A. left and clued Clete Bailey about the attempt on Deedra's life. Brent promised to have the photos of the D.A. finding the knife sent off right away, and then he had driven into North San Juan.

WHEN THE SUN SANK behind North Ledge Range and the heat of the day vanished in the cool breeze from the north that riffled tree leaves, Gavin, Brent, and Deedra sat outside the old church making plans to visit Crucible the next morning. The men didn't leave until Deedra was safe inside the old church with the latch in place. A large rock was placed against the door so that it couldn't be opened without making a lot of noise.

After giving her orders to scream as loud as she could if anyone tried to break in, they left her to rest. Gavin had tried to get her to move to the old hotel, but she had resisted, still vaguely planning to trap the killer. Alone she was bait, in the hotel nothing like what she had in mind would work. Unless, of course, Derryck Evans was the killer.

IT WAS NOT YET daylight when Deedra climbed into Brent's 4-wheel rig, and they headed out the old stage road toward the draw where they could cross over into Crucible Valley. The early morning air was clear. Here and there white-tailed deer bounded between scant vegetation and boulders. Birds were on the wing, twittering in warning at their approach. They reached the bend where the stage road veered off to the northwest. It was there that Gavin told Brent to turn east through a draw that showed signs of erosion and landslides. On each side were tall cliffs of mica and gneiss, and porphyry boulders against which vegetation huddled as if the one could not exist without the other.

At the top of the pass, Gavin told Brent to stop. "I heard Dr. Robbins say he saw Gregg search around this draw several times after leaving the dig early."

"Was Robbins suspicious of that?" Deedra asked.

"No. Just told Von Kraus that Gregg hiked this way after Von Kraus asked where Gregg had gone. They had finished excavating the first mixosaur and the digging was halted for a few days while they fitted the fossilized bones into place. That left Gregg free to pursue his own interests." He sighed. "Shelley Muldoon says Rhonda disappeared several times right about that time. Gregg might have met her somewhere. Rhonda was devious enough to have followed Gregg, though. And unless Gregg tells us, we'll probably never know. No one has admitted seeing them together. But those young people get involved in their art, and they don't take in what's going on around them."

"I think Gregg has discovered something important up here. Something he doesn't want anyone, the scientists in particular, to find out about. If he found something important, then someone might have a motive to frame him. Might even have killed Rhonda by mistake. She was a tall woman, wasn't she?"

"Yes," Gavin replied.

"The killer might have thought it was Gregg," Deedra persisted.

Gavin frowned. "I really don't think anything that Gregg found is the motive for Rhonda's murder. However, we can't overlook any clue.

"Let's spread out here and look for signs of anything that has been disturbed lately," Gavin instructed.

They parted to search the area near the top of the pass. Deedra, limping and hobbling, was certain they wouldn't find anything, though wasn't yet ready to tell Gavin that she was planning to set a trap for the killer. The fewer who knew about it the better. Now it was a personal vendetta between her and the killer. After contemplation, she concluded that Rhonda's killer had seen Alfred, either after he entered the alley or as he left, and was afraid Alfred would divulge that information. Had Alfred tried to blackmail the killer? Perhaps Mary Jane had taken advantage of Rhonda's murder to get rid of her husband. Mary Jane had a definite cruel streak, and Alfred might have had a large insurance policy with double-indemnity. Whatever the reason, it took a cold, calculating person to kill Alfred within a few yards of where the sheriff had been standing talking to them. That characteristic would fit all the scientists, Derryck, perhaps Mark Saylen, and Mary Jane. After a moment's reflection, Deedra included Shelley Muldoon on that list. It was always possible that she lived out one of her murder mysteries. The list of suspects was a long one.

Their search was unsuccessful. The canyon was different than North Ledge Valley: more rugged, the creek there deeper, swifter, the canyon narrower. Situated between North Ledge Range, and the crags of a broken volcanic rim that had sheered off, tall cliffs rose straight up like the walls of modern skyscrapers. It was a box canyon; the only escape was across the pass into North Ledge Valley.

Crucible was a shambled ruin. There were relics everywhere, remnants of blue granite cooking utensils, old insulators from an ancient telegraph line, the old "cheater" whiskey bottles. Deedra felt sad knowing weather and time would eventually mean its final destruction. Unlike North Ledge, Crucible had only one street with no alleys. The creek paralleled the street, then disappeared into a cavern. It was impossible to follow it.

"Where does that creek resurface?" Deedra asked Gavin.

"It feeds into Ledge Lake on the other side of that far ridge." He pointed to a sharp scarp miles to the south.

They searched the one remaining cabin where Deedra found a scarf with the initials V.P. embroidered on it. Evidently Valerie and Gregg had met there to avoid Mary Jane's and Rhonda's snooping.

Deedra wondered if they were lovers. Gregg, unlike Brent, didn't feel the need for conquest. His relationship with Valerie might not have progressed to that stage. If he loved her, he might not have tried to take advantage.

"So Gregg and Valerie met here," Gavin muttered.

Neither Brent nor Deedra felt called upon to make a comment.

Only the relics of a once thriving town, an old apple squeezer, and everywhere the crucibles that had made the crude assays of gold the early miners had found were there to see. Deedra gathered up a few for her collection. Brent took photos for future stories, and then they climbed into the rig and headed north following the creek.

They continued beyond the place where they had crossed over the draw. There were mine tailings on the backsides of Feather and Mica mountains, but the others were cliffs of porphyry rock with no mines and no possible way of scaling.

"I can't remember ever seeing such steep cliffs," Gavin stared at the cliff with a look of awe.

The canyon ended where the narrow fissure turned east, and the creek disappeared beyond huge boulders.

Crucible's residents really did have only one way in and one way out, and they had to depend on North Ledge Valley and its people for their survival.

Brent backed the rig, drove up a slope and around a pillar of rock, then down beside the creek again. It was when they neared the draw leading over to North Ledge that a bullet whined overhead, ricocheted off a boulder, and pinged against the left rear fender. Before the echo of the shot resounded up and down the canyon, Brent wheeled behind a cluster of boulders and straggling vegetation.

"Keep down!" Brent shouted.

Gavin cursed and trained his binoculars on the slopes above.

While Gavin and Brent looked up the mountainside for a glimpse of the sniper, Deedra studied the area further down toward Mica Mountain. Had the sniper only tried to frighten them or was it another attempt on her life? There was no movement up on the ridge, and whoever had been there was long gone. Still, they waited a long time before venturing over the draw.

"It might only have been someone like Derryck Evans playing a trick," Brent suggested.

"Hmm," Gavin replied, his anger plain.

Though they stayed behind the boulders for the better part of an hour, the sniper didn't show. Finally they drove over the pass into North Ledge Valley without further incident. They were silent, on edge, carefully scrutinizing every boulder and clump of trees.

Brent drove up to the dig. The scientists were all there. Gregg was busy recording the geologic strata. Surprisingly, Mary Jane was there watching Gregg with a smoldering gaze that he was obviously trying to ignore.

Gavin didn't question whether any of them had wandered away in the past hour or two. For the time being, they had decided not to say anything about the shooting. Gavin hoped the sniper would give himself away.

In North Ledge the artist and writers were all scattered along the banks of Jackson Creek, and only Frank Shundo was missing.

The sound of an approaching vehicle echoed about the old town, alerting them to the arrival of the sheriff's deputy. Gavin met him in front of his office while Deedra and Brent looked on from the shade of a tall pine tree growing at the side of the stage station. Gavin handed the deputy a sealed report for the District Attorney. He jotted something down in a notebook belonging to the deputy. After a few minutes of conversation the deputy departed, raising a cloud of dust that slowly settled. The hum of the engine faded as it rounded the bend on North San Juan Road.

Gavin sat on the ground beside them and opened the dossiers on the suspects furnished by the police and the District Attorney's office.

After reading the printouts, Gavin told them, "They all have motives to kill Rhonda Adams." He gestured about the town, but his gaze settled on Mary Jane's abode. "Rhonda might have been done in by Alfred. They were cousins."

He leafed through another paper. "Rhonda Adams was convicted in a criminal case several years ago, spent time in the women's prison at Tehachapi. She was older than we thought. Gregg knew about the prison thing because it was his college chum that Rhonda robbed…at gunpoint. It was before he married Mary Jane, however. Her real name was Rhonda Shepley."

"Wow," Brent muttered.

"Yeah, interesting, ain't it?" Gavin grinned.

"By the way, the D.A. conducted an inquest in absentia on Alfred Shepley using all the depositions he had taken up here. Eliminates the need for any of us to attend the pretrial in the city. The D.A. doesn't want me to leave here just in case something else happens, and he doesn't want to arouse the scientists' ire. It's politically in his best interests not to anger the universities."

"That Narkette knows where the votes are!" Brent laughed.

Gavin nodded. "Shelley Muldoon has known Gregg since college and was even engaged to him until he got mixed up with Rhonda. They couldn't find out if she knew Mary Jane or Alfred, though. Evidently Shelley hadn't met Frank Shundo before moving here. Now, it's reported that Shelley was heartbroken when Rhonda broke up her engagement to Gregg. And she has never married. Very sharp gal. Graduated summa cum laude. She's capable of planning out a murder like Rhonda's and hiding all those knives. Mystery writers write about things like that but I've never heard of any of them actually killing anyone. If Rhonda had interfered with Shelley's writing that would be another story. Shelley might have resented Rhonda's interference with the young people here. Admittedly that's a very weak motive."

Deedra and Brent nodded agreement.

"Valerie Penrose is the mystery woman. She has wealthy parents back east. Took her mother's maiden name when she moved out here. Apparently she had never met Gregg until she moved up here. It's one of those cases where the kid wants to do her own thing. Her parents are just waiting for her to get it out of her system and return east." Gavin paused to take a deep breath.

"Mark Saylen has had several science fiction books and articles published, though his ex-wife got all the money. He moved up here so she couldn't find him. Then he took a pen name. His ex-wife has remarried, and, get this, lives in a house Rhonda owned. Now, if the ex-wife set Rhonda to spying on Mark, it could create a sticky wicket. Mark could have known Rhonda before moving up here, though we haven't found any proof of that."

Gavin took another deep breath. "Now, there's Derryck Evans. No use saying that I don't suspect him, because I do. I think Derryck killed them. He's really spaced out."

"That's no real motive, Gavin," Brent replied.

"I know. It's just a hunch. Those characters usually end up doing something bizarre." Again Gavin paused as if thinking of Derryck as the killer. Then he shook his head and continued. "Zach Johnson is angry with Gregg Dancer because he's in love with Valerie Penrose himself. He resents Gregg's attentions to Valerie, and he detested Alfred Shepley almost as much as he did Rhonda Adams. We've not found anything that connects him to the couple previously. He's a very quiet guy. He may have observed more than we know from those studio windows, and being quiet does not guarantee that he didn't commit the murders. Murderers are very often quiet, reserved people."

Deedra glanced up at the old hotel and even at that very moment Zach was watching through his studio window as if he knew they were talking about him.

"Mary Jane," the sheriff continued, "has the obvious motives, the characteristics of a husband killer. She could have been furious at Rhonda's attempts to attract Gregg since she was trying to attract him again herself."

"We always," Deedra remarked, "get around to Mary Jane."

Gavin nodded. "Gregg Dancer is the only one we have circumstantial evidence against, but his motives seem obtuse. He had a destructive affair with Rhonda and he detested Alfred. I can see him killing Alfred but not Rhonda."

Gavin consulted his list again. "The scientists seem to have the weakest of motives. It's the mixosaur bone beside Rhonda's body that drags them into it, though I find it difficult to fit any of them into the role of killer. Alfred may have aroused murderous anger at the site, but what connection did that have to Rhonda? Then there's Frank Shundo who is the unknown entity. No known connection with Rhonda or Alfred Shepley. Frank did know that Mary Jane was Gregg's ex-wife. The main suspicion against Frank seems to be that he was wandering around at the murder times, no one knows where, so he had the opportunity."

"I don't know, Gavin," Deedra reminded, "all those scientists have cold analytical minds. This killer is a very cool customer. Didn't let our presence within yards of that alley deter him from killing Alfred."

"That's sure the truth. Bold and daring!" Gavin replied.

"Now, where does this all lead us?" Brent inquired.

"It tells us more about these people and gives me leads on what questions to ask them," Gavin replied, folding the printouts as if he was about to put them away.

"Does the report tell you where those young people lived before they moved up here, about their families and what they did for a living?" Deedra wanted to learn everything Gavin knew.

"Shelley Muldoon was born in Los Angeles County. She's from an old California family. Her grandfather's family crossed the plains in a wagon train and were actually some of the first settlers there. Nothing mysterious in her background. Only the fact that she was engaged to Gregg Dancer years ago even gives her the slightest motive to kill Rhonda." Gavin sighed again. "Zach Johnson has the same type background. Old California family, nothing mysterious, attended Los Angeles schools. Good student, attended art school in L.A. until he ran out of money. That doesn't mean he didn't know Rhonda, just that we haven't found any connection there."

"Have you got a warrant to search those studios?" Deedra asked.

"No. I can't search them. The D.A. already conducted that part of the investigation. I don't really know if they found anything important. He is sometimes reluctant to share information with me."

"Did he find any mineral samples?" Deedra asked.

Gavin gave her a sharp glance. "What makes you ask that?"

Deedra shrugged. "I just wondered if anyone has found anything up here besides the mixosaur."

"Yes. The scientists have mineral samples over there. I don't know what they are, though."

"Let's try to place where everyone was at the time of the murders," Brent suggested, changing the subject.

"All the young people were down at Jackson Creek.

Frank Shundo was up on Mercury Mountain. The scientists were in their quarters. Actually, Mary Jane is the only one without an alibi for Alfred's murder. However, anyone could have snuck up Dead Man's Alley long enough to stab Alfred. Both Rhonda and Alfred were stabbed in the back, both in the same alley. The same M.O. for the killer. The only difference between them is that mixosaur bone at the scene of Rhonda's murder. If Rhonda had been carrying it, she might have been visiting with someone from the site. If the murderer dropped it, then was unable to find it in the dark, it's a vital clue."

"Remember, Gavin, Frank wasn't up on Mercury Mountain. Don't you remember that he returned, went into his place, and then in a few minutes went out again? We assumed that he was going to the creek to wash up." She sighed. "With no street lights and everyone having to use outdoor plumbing, it's impossible to say that anyone has an airtight alibi."

"That's right. It was during Rhonda's murder that Frank was up on Mercury Mountain. He said he was anyway," Gavin frowned thoughtfully.

"That still makes Gregg Dancer major suspect for Rhonda's murder and Mary Jane chief suspect for killing Alfred," Brent murmured.

"Yes." Gavin glanced about the deserted street as if he thought ghosts lingered there and were somehow going to assist him.

"I'm going up on that ridge to see if that sniper left a calling card. I think he only wanted to frighten Deedra and me away, perhaps keep us away from the mixosaur dig."

"It might only have been another red herring to implicate someone from the dig, Brent. Just like placing that mixosaur bone next to Rhonda's body could be. It's as if someone wants us to look at the scientists, not at the artists," Deedra suggested.

"Yeah," Gavin replied. "It makes me suspect Derryck Evans even more."

"I'll park my rig on this side of the dig. I don't want the professors up there to know that I'm anywhere around," Brent told them.

"Is Frank up on Mercury Mountain?"

Deedra pointed to mine tailings where they could see a man moving about on the outcropping near the old mine. "I think that's Frank."

Gavin peered through his binoculars. "Yep, that's Frank. He's been staying up on that side of the mountain for days now. I wonder if he's found something important."

"There's cinnabar there. He's trying to determine whether there's enough to make mining profitable," Deedra told him.

"Cinnabar?" Gavin looked at her with a surprised grin.

"Yes, it's a mercury mineral. See that reddish-colored outcrop right there where Frank's walking? That's cinnabar. Must have been enough there to cause the mountain to get its name."

Gavin studied the mountain through his binoculars with more interest. "Mercury, eh? That's kind of valuable, isn't it?"

"I'm sure it is," Deedra replied, her eyes following Frank's progress on the mountain.

"See you two later," Brent said. "I'm off to see if I can learn something about that sniper." Brent poured gas into his rig and then headed out the old stage road in a cloud of dust.

If it hadn't been for her injured ankle, Deedra would have begged to go along.

They watched in silence as Brent's car roared along Stagecoach Road then disappeared after crossing the ford over Jackson Creek.

Deedra had an uncanny feeling that Brent had just driven off into danger. She shook herself. Silly imagination! She couldn't let that sniper cause her to fear every move they made. Nevertheless, Deedra felt a sudden coldness around her heart.

ELEVEN

DEEDRA LIMPED UP to the old church to read Gregg's book on minerals by John Sinkankas, who was an authority on gemology. Sinkankas had cut and faceted many of the valuable gems in the Smithsonian Institute's gem collection. She was intrigued by Gregg's drawings and had a suspicion that she had seen something similar in Sinkankas' books. She was also curious why her attacker had taken the gems. Did that person realize the significance of those gemstones?

Deedra compared the drawings Gregg had drawn with the one she found on page 190 of *Gemstones and Minerals.* Sure enough, the drawings were similar, the gems in almost the exact "in situ." That was why the drawings had looked so familiar. Obviously Gregg had discovered a valuable mineral deposit.

The scientists would recognize it as similar to the Himalaya pegmatite deposit of Mesa Grande, San Diego County, California, and immediately know of its importance. If the killer was one of the young artists or writers, they probably wouldn't have understood the sketches. The question was had the killer seen Gregg's sketches when he took Gregg's knife? That would precipitate a search and perhaps the killer's attack on her was for the gemstones and not because her attacker thought she had dangerous knowledge of his identity.

Mary Jane could have figured out what the sketches meant, perhaps she even showed them to Alfred, who most certainly would have realized what they were.

Deedra read John Sinkankas' description again, sitting on the floor and leaning against the rough planks. The thing was, the killer did not know where the gem deposit was and that lack of knowledge was going to allow her to try and trap him.

She took paper from her news reporter's case then drew a map. Not of the mine, however. This map was to lead the killer astray, send him looking in a place where his actions would give him away.

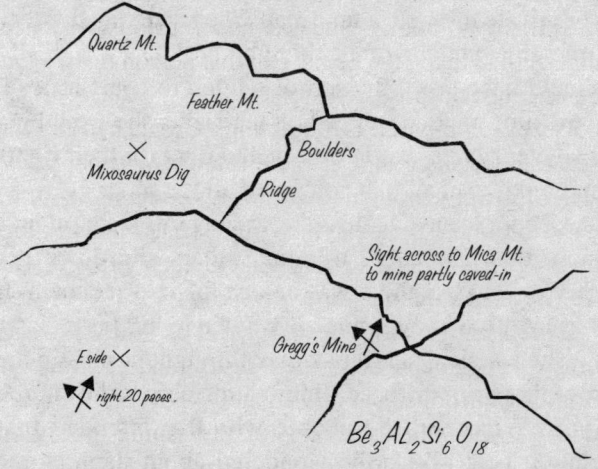

Be3 AL2 Si6 O18

This was the formula for the mineral beryl which includes the gemstones, emerald, aquamarine, and other valuable gemstones.

DEEDRA HAD TO WAIT to spring her trap. Her wounds were still too painful and she wanted to be able to follow the killer. Somehow she had to prove that Gregg Dancer and Frank Shundo were not guilty of the murders. Every time she thought of Frank's expression, that deep hurt, the look of hopelessness, she cringed. She had to figure out when and how to let the killer know she had a map to Gregg's discovery. It must not look like a trap. Deedra was careful to use the correct terminology and symbols on the map just in case one of the scientists was the killer. If it was incorrect, they would immediately suspect Gavin had something to do with it and shy away. Deedra had once caught a man who was snooping into her private life with a fake map. She had to laugh every time she thought of it, though she knew she really should have taken the son-of-a-bitch to court instead. Next time anyone stepped on her rights she would get a lawyer right away. People had to fight for their rights and reporters had to be on guard all the time.

Deedra leaned against the wall again. Her arm hurt more than she cared to admit. Tears slid down her cheeks now that there was no one there to see them. It was awful to know someone wanted to kill her.

She watched sunlight streak through the slits in the roof throwing diffused illumination across the church floor. What had the people who had attended that church been like? She wondered about them, some walking that long rough road over the pass from Crucible, their faith alive and strong. Lost in contemplation, Deedra drifted into slumber. Her wounds had taken a toll on her strength.

The map to trap the killer lay on the floor beside her.

"DEEDRA! DEEDRA! Are you in there?" Valerie Penrose's voice pierced her deep slumber.

"Yes, I'm here," she croaked.

She felt around the floor for the map. It was gone. Fear flowed through her. The door to the lean-to was open. Through the cracks in the rough planking she saw a shadow flitter alongside the church hurrying toward Jackson Creek.

Deedra realized that Valerie's arrival had probably saved her life. The killer had actually been in the church, had stolen the map, and had been close enough to kill her.

"Shelley and I want you to have supper with us," Valerie shouted.

"Yes, thanks. I'll be along in a few minutes. I need to freshen up."

"Right. We'll be expecting you then. Do you know where Brent is?"

Cold fear shot through her. "No. Hasn't he returned from scouting along the ridge above the dig?"

"No. His car isn't here."

"Tell Gavin right away!" Deedra's voice wavered with fear.

Quickly she relocked the door to the lean-to, ran a comb through her blonde curls, and added lipstick, noting the frightened look in her eyes. Her irises were dark with awful premonition.

As Deedra limped toward North Ledge, Gavin's 4-wheel rig roared across the bridge toward her.

"Stay there, Deedra. We're going to look for Brent."

Frank and Zach Johnson rode along with Gavin. Before the dust settled, Steven Robbins' 4-wheel rig roared up the road after Gavin with Mark Saylen and

Derryck Evans clinging to the sides. They had jumped aboard as Steven drove by.

Drs. Von Kraus and Drake searched up and down Jackson Creek. It was in an eerie twilight that they sloshed about the creek, probing deeper pools and places where the brush grew at the very edge of the water. The beams from flashlights and lanterns refracted off the water with shiny luminescence, throwing weird shadows into the darkness. Their sloshing noises accentuated the sound of locusts and the twittering of disturbed night birds. More than anything else, the search pointed to their mortality.

Deedra shuddered.

She limped back to the old church where she prayed that Brent would be found alive. Her prayers didn't relieve her fears, however. She was reminded that night how quickly darkness fell in that old town. It was as if a curtain had suddenly closed. Only once during the night did Deedra recall the missing map. Later it was her only excuse for not telling Gavin Blair about it.

The men found Brent's 4-wheel rig at the base of the ridge where Feather Mountain and Mica Mountain joined. It was parked in a clump of trees, explaining why the professors hadn't seen it when they returned from the dig that afternoon. From there the men began an ineffectual and dangerous search.

Deedra and the other women watched the moving lights as the men went about the mountainside. It was like the flicker of fireflies, first here, then there. Occasionally the echo of their shouts wafted down the canyon, poignant, haunting. Was it, she thought, the call for a soul already lost? She swallowed a lump of fear in her throat that threatened her breathing. She mustn't lose her grip now when Brent really needed her; she had to think logically, cautiously.

After hours and hours during which they called and searched, and searched and called, Gavin brought the men back to North Ledge to rest until daylight. They had left Brent's 4-wheel rig where it was just in case Brent returned to it.

Deedra called Clete Bailey on Gavin's police radio. Clete wanted to send a search team, but Gavin persuaded him that they had adequate help. He added that people on the mountains with their dangerous old mines posed additional hazards for searchers.

Clete asked, "What do you think happened, Deedra?"

"I think the killer trapped Brent somewhere. Then he came to the old church intending to kill me but Valerie Penrose happened along just then and frightened him away."

Deedra glanced at the men who were seated alongside the Wells Fargo station drinking hot coffee.

Lowering her voice, Deedra continued, "I drew a false map to trap the killer and when I woke up the killer had already stolen it from my room! I really wasn't ready to spring the trap just yet. I don't have any idea who did it, though a vague suspicion is beginning to form in my mind."

"Deedra, you do the damndest things!" Clete spluttered.

"I get the stories, don't I? Besides, I have a personal vendetta with this creep. He's tried to kill me and may have already killed Brent!" She choked up, tears scalding her cheeks. She brushed them away; she couldn't give in to grief yet.

If Gavin hadn't been deep in conversation with Mark Saylen at the time Deedra rang off, she would have told him right then about the map. In her worry about Brent, she forgot it and each time it came to mind, Gavin was engaged in some other pursuit.

That night was a long hell.

Daylight outlined the weary lines on the men's faces, and the frightened looks on the women's. The District Attorney arrived right after Gavin and all the men had set out on the search again.

"What in hell is going on here, Deedra Masefield?" The D.A. was in a shouting mood as he leaped from the police vehicle.

"Brent went out searching for a sniper that shot at us yesterday morning over in Crucible."

"Crucible? Where the hell is Crucible?" the D.A. muttered angrily.

Deedra told Narkette what had taken place and heard him order the officers to join in the search.

Narkette took over Gavin's office, ordering all of the women in town to gather there for an interrogation. As he ushered them in he gave Deedra a sharp look, nodding toward the hotel, and then winked. Deedra knew he wanted her to search the rooms while the women were occupied answering questions.

She waited at the back of the group until everyone was involved in answering questions, then slipped out passing Frank's house, pausing long enough to make certain she hadn't been observed. She then scurried to the old Frontier Hotel.

The downstairs was gloomy, and echoed hollowly as she crossed to the stairs. She limped up them two at a time, trying to favor her sprained ankle, knowing she had to hurry or get caught there. From the balcony she noted that everyone was still inside the old Wells Fargo station with the D.A.

The second floor stairs was on the Boothill Alley side, the third floor at the far north end facing Frank's place. Anyone going upstairs had to pass the rooms of those living on the second floor. This caused Deedra to wonder if Rhonda had kept track of everyone's activities.

Mark Saylen's studio was neat, nothing suspicious there, no guns, no books on mineralogy or geology.

Deedra was more interested in Shelley Muldoon's studio. Being a writer herself, she was curious about Shelley's lifestyle. There was nothing in her rooms to connect her to Rhonda or Alfred Shepley, and after a hasty glance across the balcony toward the D.A.'s temporary office she hastened on to Rhonda's studio.

The porno Rhonda wrote was nauseating. She had illustrated it with snapshots and photos of doubtful and suspicious origin. In her bedroom, Deedra found a large crystal of tourmaline, quite a valuable one with the typical tourmaline coloring. She wondered who had given it to Rhonda. Had Gregg? Further search didn't turn up a rifle or books on mineralogy.

She heard a noise in the hall, but when she glanced out, didn't see anyone, though decided that she would finish snooping in Rhonda's room another time, and hastily limped up to the third floor.

From Zach Johnson's window she saw that Narkette was still holding court. He had a captive audience.

Zach's studio was as neat as he was. There were no

guns, no books on mineralogy, nor did she find any gemstones from Gregg's mine.

She glanced out the window in time to see Valerie and Shelley walking toward the hotel.

She hurried down to Rhonda's room and shut the door just as the hotel's front door squeaked open. Deedra swore, and then decided that while she was there she might as well really search Rhonda's rooms. Maybe Rhonda hid some of her stuff where no could easily find it.

There were no secret drawers, nothing taped to the back of her mirror or in any of her books. Deedra stood in the center of the room trying to put herself in Rhonda's place. If she had damaging information what would she do with it? Hide it somewhere in the rough old planking? She began to poke and pry at the old boards, looking for one that seemed loose. She was almost ready to give it up when one of the boards near the ceiling moved. She was in the act of getting Rhonda's makeshift chair when Shelley opened the door.

"Oh! You scared me, Shelley!"

Shelley grinned with that Irish elfin humor. "Caught you in the act, eh?"

Deedra sighed. "Yeah. I thought I might find a clue here. And Gavin told me I could look at some of Rhonda's books."

"I doubt if you'll find anything. The police already really went over it," Shelley replied. "I hear you went to school with Gregg Dancer?"

"Yes and Frank Shundo. Someone said you were once engaged to Gregg? Is it correct that Rhonda caused you to break off your engagement?"

A look of anger flared in Shelley's eyes, and then

dimmed as she controlled her emotions. "Yes, that's true. It was a long time ago, though, and a lot of water has run under the bridge since then. Gregg's in love with Valerie now."

"Jealous?"

"At first. Then I realized that Gregg isn't really what I'm hunting for. I'm not even certain I know what that is. My writing is the most important thing to me right now."

"Did Rhonda recognize you?"

"Not at first. After Gregg started paying attention to Valerie and Rhonda tried to break that up, Gregg told her. Threatened her, really. Told Rhonda that she couldn't come between him and Valerie as she had between Gregg and me."

"The District Attorney knows about that?" When Shelly nodded, Deedra remarked, "Makes it look bad for Gregg."

"Yes. It's really as damaging as that knife," Shelley replied.

"Did Rhonda try to get anyone interested in, say an orgy, for material for her porn books?"

"Yes. Mark told her off. We all threatened to leave. She backed off then. Her invitations to all the men were quite open. Valerie had never met anyone like her, and was obviously shocked…and disgusted. You know, Deedra, it's one thing to read about such things. It's fantasy that way. Rhonda was the reality that made us all queasy."

"Did Rhonda have any visitors here?"

"No. She did leave one day with a stack of manuscripts. I suspect she met someone between here and North San Juan. She didn't have the manuscripts when she returned, and she wasn't gone long enough to have made a trip to Grass Valley."

"Was she a talented writer, Shelley?"

"She could have been, I guess. Her stuff's so filthy it's difficult to tell."

Knowing that she would get nothing further from Shelley, that she would have to finish the search another time, she gathered up a few books and Rhonda's unfinished manuscript and limped away.

WORRY FOR BRENT nearly unseated her thoughts. She felt helpless. Anxiety haunted her, nagged ceaselessly at her mind. Brent wasn't the type to just get lost in the mountains. Besides, he could see North Ledge from any of the ridges.

She went to Brent's lodgings. There was a faint smell of his aftershave lotion still clinging to the still air. She listened to her intuition and it told her Brent wasn't dead…yet.

Quickly, she bandaged her ankle, swallowed two aspirin and then placed the bottle in her jeans pocket.

Stepping onto Frontier Street, she saw Shelley Muldoon standing at her window looking off toward the mountains. What were her thoughts? Did she have any idea who the murderer was?

The street was deserted. Mary Jane had evidently returned from the dig and was shut up in her place. Was she packing, getting ready to leave North Ledge? There was obviously going to be a funeral for Alfred Shepley soon. Deedra pushed the thought from her mind. The need to find Brent was of the utmost urgency, everything else about this damn murder case could wait.

She glanced toward the mountains, saw the men wandering about the hillside like ants in search of food…and shivered.

Would the killer check to see if Brent was dead while pretending to search for him? Then make certain of it before revealing Brent's location to the others? No, she thought, the killer would have made certain the first time, would now stay away from the place where Brent was, inevitably prolonging the search.

She glanced back at the hotel, but Shelley was not at her window. Deedra went in search of the D.A. and found him searching Frank's place.

"Oh, Deedra! Find anything up at the hotel?"

"No. I didn't have a chance to look at Valerie's or Derryck's rooms. No rifle, no nothing." Deedra didn't tell the D.A. that she thought she might have located a hiding place in Rhonda's room's nor of the tourmaline crystal since it had obviously been there when the police had searched.

"I couldn't keep the women here any longer; it would seem fake," Narkette offered by way of an apology.

Deedra didn't tell him she intended to search for Brent, knowing Narkette would order her to stay in North Ledge even if he had to use the "material witness" excuse.

With added urgency, she hurried to the church where she put gas in her 4-wheel rig, placed gasoline, water, emergency rations, first aid supplies, a snake bite kit, and rope in the back seat. Hoping Shelley hadn't returned to the balcony and seen her, Deedra drove across Stagecoach Bridge, up Frontier Street, and around the Shepleys living quarters in the saloon, then angled up the ridge scattering pebbles and wisps of dust.

Shelley was at her window and frowned as she watched Deedra drive away. The D.A. hadn't been in sight, however. Deedra suspected that he was searching the scientists' quarters.

After crossing the ridge above Boothill Alley, she began the long zigzag climb up Mica Mountain, driving up at an angle, approaching it from the opposite direction that the others had taken, and the location of the mixosaur site. Though the tailings were visible from North Ledge, there were more old mines here than on the other mountains. Deedra inspected each mine for evidence that Brent had been there. The 4-wheel responded with that special pull power, the engine humming in perfect time causing Deedra to give thanks that she had the car tuned-up before leaving the city. She followed the traces of an old road which meandered up the mountain past the old mines. Occasionally she stopped and called Brent's name. The echo that answered her sounded desolate, empty.

After crossing a place where erosion had cut deep ruts, she began to stop at each mine, explore each mine shaft. She put on a hard hat with carbide lamp, carried a flashlight and a gun. Each tunnel echoed her shouts, each ominously empty. She ventured into them as far as she dared. It was slow going. There was no indication that Brent had ever been there, or of a recent cave-in.

Wearily she drove on, her strength waning, plagued by exhaustion. She hadn't slept the night before, and her arm and ankle hurt. Even her bones felt weary. At last she was forced to sit in the shade of the rig, eat a candy bar for quick energy and take another aspirin for pain. The cold water from her canteen was refreshing.

It was a very hot July day. The sun was high overhead in midday heat and there was no shade anywhere. Perspiration dried quickly on Deedra's forehead. She ached for a cool place in the shade to rest, but the need to find Brent spurred her on.

Each mineshaft was an inviting shady coolness. When she stepped back into the day's heat, it was like a sudden blow to the head, and the bright sunlight caused her to squint. Her ankle and arm became a wearisome burden. She paused long enough to swallow another aspirin.

It must have been after 3:00 when Deedra discovered the caved-in mine shaft. It was close to a mine on top of the mountain, and it had caved in during the last few hours. She knew that from the traces of moisture when she ran the earth between her fingers.

Her heart thumped with fear. She forced herself to remain calm, to think logically. If Brent was trapped there, giving way to hysterics was not going to help him. She glanced above the mine's location to the peak, then sighted down the slope. There was no sign of landslide or any shift in the earth.

She took a shovel from the side rack and carefully dug several feet into the newly moved earth. About ten feet inside the tunnel her shovel hit a fallen timber. Complete mine collapse! She groaned as a wave of grief swept over her. Then suddenly she shoveled faster, crying, shouting Brent's name. But her efforts were useless. It would take heavy equipment to open up the tunnel.

She tried to reach Gavin on her C.B., but it didn't work up there, and Gavin was evidently away from his rig. Even if she managed to reach him, there wasn't the proper equipment to dig Brent out. She glanced up at the ridge again, then suddenly recalled that old mines often intersected, that often one mine shaft tunneled into another. Usually they tunneled toward the main vein from several directions, each mine owner thinking they had discovered a separate mine, but all tunneling to a central deposit within the heart of the mountain.

Using her compass, she marked the line location on a page of her notebook, then drew lines from a seam of gold she imagined in the mountain. Studying the peak she recalled seeing deep shafts going straight down into the bowels of the mountain. Yes, there was a slight chance that the tunnels intersected. She re-checked the line, sighting off her shovel handle. She was certain the mines were at least very close together. There might be a chance of reaching Brent through the alternate mine shaft, the one going straight down into the mountain.

Shaking with fear and urgency, she shifted into the gear known to 4-wheelers as "grandma," that growly gear, that pulling gear, that slowly allowed her to climb the precarious slope. She zigzagged upward, frustrated at the length of time it took to reach the top, her head aching, her arm paining. She gritted her teeth to keep from groaning.

For the first time she realized the full depth of her feelings for Brent. She had always been in love with Deke Thomas, had only half-heartedly thought of other men. Now all her thoughts were on Brent, her fear for him the catalyst that gave her strength to do what had to be done. That fear caused her to groan aloud at intervals. It was a real test of her driving that she was able to reach the top without tipping over. She had never driven in such a dangerous place, had never actually put the 4-wheel rig to the ultimate test. She knew now that if she didn't reach the top, it would be her skill that was lacking.

The higher she got on the mountain, the cooler the breeze. It helped. She ran over unsuspecting snakes, wended the rig between clumps of mesquite, straggly junipers, and greasewood. She crossed graveled places where traction seemed impossible. Several times the 4-wheel rig tipped dangerously, though always righted itself. At last she drove onto a faint road that hadn't been used in a century. She was suddenly at the top. The old mineshaft gaped like an open wound.

She put rocks behind the wheels so the rig wouldn't suddenly take off down the mountain, then crawled to the edge of the shaft. It was an absolutely black void. The darkness caught at her in fresh terror.

"Brent! Brent! Are you down there?"

There was an eon of time when the echo of her voice resounded hollowly, seemingly lost in the labyrinths of the earth.

"Deedra! Am I dreaming?"

"Brent! Are you hurt?" Deedra tried to judge the depth of the shaft by the echo of her voice. Tears rolled down her face in relief that he was alive.

"Bruised, can't get out."

"Brent, stand near the wall of the shaft. I'll throw a light down to you."

"Okay."

Deedra took the spare hard hat with carbide lamp from the rig, and let it drop into the center of the shaft. It was a long moment before she heard the thump as it hit the ground. In a moment she saw a faint light from the depths. The tunnel was not as deep as she had feared.

"Listen! I'm going to winch you out of there. When I let the rope down, wrap it around your hands, or your waist if it's long enough. Then walk up the walls," she paused to let the echo die away. "If you walk up the walls, it will keep you from hitting the sides, take some of the weight off your shoulders."

"I heard you," Brent replied. Nevertheless, his voice sounded weak.

Deedra felt a new fear. If he had broken bones or other injuries he might not be about to be winched out.

Again she placed rocks behind the wheels as she inched forward, praying the weight of the rig wouldn't start a cave-in. When she was within a few feet of the shaft, she braked, dragged an old timber in front of the wheels to prevent it from rolling forward. Fear sent another stab through her after paying out the rope to find that it wasn't long enough to reach Brent.

"Hold on, I've got another rope."

Deedra drew up the winch rope, attached another coil of rope from the emergency supplies. She tied a knot she was taught by a Navy man in high school, another of the circle of friends that knew Gregg and Frank. Then ran the rope down the shaft.

"Can you reach it now?"

"No, it's just inches above my head."

"Damn!" Deedra returned to the rig, looking for something Brent could stand on. She was drenched in perspiration of frustration and fear. Then she began to hiccough.

She yelled down to Brent. "I've got to find something for you to stand on. Take me a few minutes."

"I can dig some earth and form a sort of platform."

"No! Don't! It might start a cave-in."

"Oh," Brent's voice had a defeated sound.

She dared not move the 4-wheel rig lest it start a cave-in, but it was difficult to hobble around on her sprained ankle which was swelling with each passing moment. On the slope there were pieces of old lumber and rough planking. A snake buzzed in its own frustration as she hobbled along, but it was out of striking distance. After Deedra threw a rock at it, the reptile slithered off into an area of large rocks. Deedra had to fight down the nausea of revulsion.

It took precious minutes for her to carry the boards up the steep slope, her injuries cumbersome, and the effort caused her to swear and groan. From her emergency kit she took a hammer and nails, and fashioned a box-like stool from the old lumber, then reinforced it by nailing a board across the top of it. She then wrapped tumbleweeds around it, hoping to keep it from breaking when she threw it down the shaft.

"Brent, stand back. I'm going to throw this stool down." She waited for the echo to die, then dropped the box into the black void hoping it wouldn't smash when it hit the bottom. The plop sound echoed up as if from another sphere.

"You okay, Brent?"

"Yes." There was a long pause. "I've got hold of the rope, but it's not long enough to tie around my waist."

"Yell when you're ready for me to start the winch." Deedra watched the flicker of Brent's carbide lamp. When he shouted, "Ready," she went to the rig and began winching Brent out of the mineshaft.

The winch groaned and screeched, the engine growled in a raspy manner. Slowly, Brent began to move upward, walking on the walls, keeping himself from swinging back and forth.

Deedra realized how painful that ascent was, how Brent must be suffering, though she didn't try to talk to him. There were long minutes when the only sounds were the squeal and hum of the engine interspersed by grunts and groans from Brent. The light from the carbide lamp allowed Deedra to watch Brent's progress, a very long time where she took only shallow breaths and kept silent, afraid any talk would divert Brent's attention and cause him to lose his grip.

Brent's foot slipped. He swung into the shaft, slowly swinging back and forth. She held her breath, praying, until he managed to slow and start walking upward again.

When Brent neared the top, she could see that blood covered his face, and dripped along with his sweat, wetting his shirt with ugly grime. His head wound looked wicked. At last he was up and over the edge, stumbling forward before Deedra could get the winch stopped.

Brent fell to the ground in front of the 4-wheel rig.

There was a sudden roar behind them. Large chunks of earth vanished into the mineshaft, creating a hollow crater around the mine.

Brent had fainted.

Deedra pushed down hysteria, she wanted to stand there and scream and sob, but Brent needed attention and they had to get away from that collapsed mine shaft. She revived him with a vial of ammonia from the first aid kit, and gave him water from her canteen. Though it was urgent to move the rig, she took the time to bandage Brent's head wound, gave him another drink of water before dragging him to it. He revived enough to get into the passenger seat, and then fainted again.

Deedra reset the emergency brake and then cautiously removed the rocks from the back wheels. With a thumping heart she began to back off the mountain peak. She was forced to turn on a sharp slant where the rig lurched in a sickening way, then fell back on all four wheels.

She was shaking so badly that she had to stop at a place where large boulders prevented them from toppling down the steep slope. She gulped water, wishing it was something stronger, something to give her added courage.

"He tried to kill me," Brent muttered.

"Who did?"

"Killer," Brent fainted again.

After cleaning and bathing Brent's face, she washed his hands, then put the canteen to his lips again. He swallowed automatically, but didn't revive. It was important right then to get water in him as rapidly as possible without making him nauseous. There were no other signs of serious injury, though he was badly scratched and bruised.

She placed a heavy jacket under his head where he leaned against the doorpost so the rough terrain wouldn't jar him anymore than necessary. She worried about concussion, knowing that it was important to keep his head immobile.

With hands that trembled from weakness and relief, she carefully shifted into low gear, then began the treacherous trek down the old switchback trail. The vehicle swayed occasionally. By swiftly turning the wheels downward instead of up, she kept it from overturning, though there were times when only by leaning against Brent did she keep the vehicle upright. It took longer to drive down the mountain than it had to drive up. She couldn't pick up speed. Never had she driven in such a dangerous area.

The terrain was rugged. She avoided the worst places whenever possible, even when it meant taking a longer route. Several times in the shade of old mine tailings she stopped and put water to Brent's lips, bathed his hands and face. Her own wounds were dull heavy aches and she was shaking with exhaustion. Finally she was forced to take more aspirin. There was a buzzing in her head that warned her against taking any more.

About halfway down the mountain, out of sight of the mixosaur dig, Brent regained consciousness long enough to say, "Deedra, don't let the killer know I'm alive."

Deedra braked to a sudden stop. Brent was right. If the killer knew he was alive, he would make another attempt to silence him. Brent was in no condition to defend himself.

She looked toward North Ledge. There was no movement, no cars indicating that the men had returned. It was too far to take Brent to Mercury Mountain without the risk of being seen. Crucible was too far away to provide him with food and water, and she would be forced to drive across the draw which would attract attention. Even the old church wasn't safe since the killer was after her, too. She studied the scene below through binoculars that had still been strapped around Brent's shoulders. On the far side of Boothill Ridge was an old mine and an adobe shack. A creek meandered off to the southwest. The hut would do until she and Gavin could think of something else. Since the killer thought Brent was trapped in that mine, he wouldn't go around looking for him, though someone else might stumble upon him.

She gave North Ledge another look, detected no movement, and drove down into a gully out of sight of North Ledge, then crossed to the far side of Boothill Ridge.

Brent groaned with pain as the vehicle ran over rocks and through scaly ruts. She didn't stop, couldn't stop. Brent's life depended on her getting him into that old adobe hut without being seen.

The murderer would kill Deedra just for finding Brent, and she knew that both their lives depended on her skill in hiding Brent…and in being able to keep him alive until Gavin could arrange to get him out of North Ledge. "I've got to trap that damn killer before he traps us," she muttered.

TWELVE

DEEDRA WAS IN the old church when the exhausted men drove into North Ledge that evening. Their search, of course, had been unsuccessful. They were weary, frustrated, defeated.

Deedra experienced a flash of guilt knowing that Brent was alive, and then the thought that one of them was a murderer, a vicious killer, drove that feeling away. She had hidden Brent in the adobe hut, left emergency rations, water, flashlight, and a gun. Brent had told her he hadn't seen the killer's face.

It seemed centuries before she got to talk to Gavin alone. His conference with the District Attorney on the police radio went on endlessly. The other men went off in search of food and rest.

Gavin was dead tired. Dark circles smudged his gray eyes and his clothes were stained with dirt and sweat.

"Gavin," Deedra burst out when he tried to ignore her, "I just have to speak to you alone!" She called attention to Brent's black news reporter notebook in her hand.

"Right." Gavin gestured toward his vehicle. "It's just that I'm so damn tired, but I do need to call home and the reception here is lousy tonight. Let's drive out North San Juan Road."

Wincing from the bruises of her dangerous venture,

Deedra climbed aboard thinking how blissful it would be just to close her eyes and let oblivion take over.

"Only damn place where I can be certain we won't be overheard," Gavin muttered as they traveled. He parked just beyond the ridge where they couldn't be seen by anyone in North Ledge.

"Tell me," Gavin demanded in a quiet tone law officers use when they know they are about to learn something important.

"I found Brent. The killer hit him over the head and dragged him into an old mine shaft. Then deliberately caused the shaft to collapse. Brent crawled through to a side tunnel, then that tunnel collapsed behind him. Luckily the second tunnel was connected to that big mine on top of Mica Mountain. I winched him out just seconds before it collapsed. I think Brent's got a concussion, and maybe internal injuries. Brent asked me to hide him from the killer."

"Did Brent see the killer?" Gavin's voice took on cold analytical anger.

"No. He kept losing consciousness so I couldn't really question him. He's eaten and had water. I don't know how he had the strength to hold onto that rope while he was being hauled up out of there!" Deedra's voice broke on recalling the moments when only the screech of the winch broke the mountain of silence. "The best thing for him now is rest. I left food and water, a hunting knife and a gun, so if the killer goes calling, he might get killed himself."

"Where did you get the gun?"

"I keep one in my rig. Don't worry. I have a permit to carry it."

"How did you know where to look for him?" Gavin leaned back against the seat, exhausted, relieved.

"I just recalled how those old mines were, how they often tunneled into someone else's mine shaft. It was the cause of many fights between mine owners in the old days. I looked for a caved-in mine. When I found it and realized that it had happened within the last few hours, I guessed that Brent was trapped inside. What better way for the killer to get rid of him? I saw that old mine up on Mica Mountain the other day, and knew it was deep, that it went straight down into the heart of the mountain. I worked on the theory that the mines tunneled into each other, that they tunneled toward the center."

Deedra went into detail, telling Gavin how she had winched Brent out of the mineshaft, how it had collapsed, and the dangerous trek down the mountainside.

After Gavin reported to Narkette, Deedra called Clete with the news that Brent was alive, he promised to hold the story for and get in touch with Brent's newspaper.

"Nothing must panic the killer into another attempt on Brent's life," Deedra told Clete Bailey. "His safety depends on the killer thinking that he's trapped inside that old mine."

"Only forty-eight hours then," Clete replied, abruptly hanging up before she could object or agree.

Deedra felt stabs of fury with Clete, forced herself into a quiet mode for a time calming her sense of outrage.

Later, she asked Gavin, "Can we keep them from finding Brent?"

"I'll keep the men up on the mountain tomorrow, and we'll discover that cave-in which should reassure the killer that his scheme has worked. Then we'll call off the search, and I'll pretend to order heavy equipment in to dig out that cave-in. That way I'll be around North Ledge where I can keep an eye on everyone. The professors will hot-foot it up to the mixosaur dig, of course. You'll have to keep an eye on the women, watch where they go. Perhaps you can set up a surveillance point somewhere."

"I thought about driving out toward North San Juan, and circling around so I could get food and supplies to Brent. I can only do that occasionally, though, or someone might get suspicious."

Gavin nodded. "If it wouldn't alert the killer, I'd move Brent into my quarters. Perhaps when he's able to withstand the trip you should drive him back to the city." Gavin suggested. "Yes. That's what we'd better do. Brent is helpless with that head wound. We need to get him clear out of here. We might even get a deputy to drive him out, then you wouldn't have to leave which is bound to cause questions. The killer will be watching everyone, questioning everything, every move. Anything the least out of the ordinary will attract his attention, cause him suspicion."

"Any ideas about the identity of this killer?" Deedra noted the weary sag of Gavin's normally stern features.

"I don't think it's Frank Shundo. And I'm certain that it isn't Gregg. I keep wondering about Derryck Evans because he's so spaced out. It would take someone like that to pull that cave-in stunt. I don't think it's a woman's work, although Mary Jane is certainly capable of that kind of cruelty."

"I don't think she's strong enough to have loaded Brent into that ore cart, and I doubt Derryck is patho-

logically insane. Derryck likes to shock people, like a
gleeful teenager. Instead of graffiti and racing about in
stolen cars, he paints out his fantasies; he doesn't act
them out. It's the ones who repress their fantasies that
commit mass murders and all the rest of it."

"Yeah, that's what I've heard," Gavin replied in a
doubtful tone. "I guess I'm just prejudiced against
Derryck. I've never been in a studio that set my nerves
on edge like that one."

"Frankly, Gavin, I found Rhonda's studio more
disgusting."

Gavin laughed. "Yep, it's that all right!" He laughed
again. "Let's get back to North Ledge and get some rest.
The killer isn't going to hunt for Brent tonight, and I
want to be alert tomorrow."

"Yes. I'm really tired." Deedra had forgotten about
the fake map and the fact that the killer had stolen it.

NORTH LEDGE WAS LIKE a silent tomb when they drove
up to the old church and Gavin watched until she was
safely inside with a rock pushed against the door. She
listened to the sound of the engine as Gavin crossed the
bridge. Then a deep hush when Gavin shut off the engine.

The night birds took up their quavering trill and the
crickets blended into the night serenade with a ratchet
and hum. Up on the mountain a coyote yelped out to his
comrades, and an owl hooted mournfully.

Deedra wondered if the killer was awake, lying in his
bed planning his next move.

THIRTEEN

DEEDRA AWOKE to a gloomy day. Clouds darkened the sky; a ponderous thunderstorm loomed over Mica Mountain. The air was heavy with ozone that foretold of rain. The temperature had dropped dramatically overnight. Deedra shivered as she dressed, and wondered if Brent had kept warm during the night. Since he was suffering from shock it was dangerous for him to get chilled. He needed a sleeping bag and she had left him only a blanket and two jackets.

After gulping a breakfast of soda crackers and cheese, Deedra limped off toward North Ledge arriving in time to talk to Gavin before the men left for the search.

"I'm taking them up on Mica Mountain right away so we can find that caved-in mine, and then I'll call off the search before the storm hits," Gavin murmured. "You watch the others, and be careful! The killer might be a woman, you know."

"Go slow, Gavin. Find that caved-in mine as casually as you can."

Gavin led the convoy of vehicles up Dead Man's Alley, and then they roared over Boothill Ridge. The chill seemed to prevent dust, and instead of the puffy cloud which usually followed in the wake of the rigs, only the smoke from exhaust was left to dissipate in the cool morning air. The group followed the ridge until they reached the base of Mica Mountain where they spread out to search a wide area.

Deedra watched Valerie and Shelley stroll up the street deep in conversation and disappear into the Frontier Hotel.

Mary Jane was seated on her front porch smoking a cigarette, her face taut, her gaze hard and unrelenting in the early morning light. She stared at Deedra and when Deedra returned the stare, Mary Jane crushed out her cigarette then walked into Dead Man's Alley gazing toward the vehicles up on Mica Mountain. When she turned to look at Deedra again, there was a deep frown etched on her face.

Deedra leaned against Gavin's office waiting for Mary Jane to go inside her abode so she could take supplies to Brent. Her anxiety for him caused restless frustration. Only the thought of protecting him from the killer kept her from rushing to his side.

Mary Jane walked up and down the alley, angry, seemingly frustrated, her steps erratic and uneven, as if she wished herself somewhere else or wished Deedra would go away. After a time she tired and went inside the church.

Deedra waited.

Sure enough, a few minutes later, Mary Jane reappeared, smoking another cigarette, obviously irritated to find Deedra still there, then she walked to Boothill Alley where she stood and stared off toward Mica Mountain. Did she know where the caved-in mine was? Was that what caused her uneasiness?

Still Deedra waited.

At last Mary Jane tired of the game, tossed her cigarette into the dust of Frontier Street, and went into the hotel. In a few minutes Deedra saw her at the window of Rhonda's room. She gave Deedra a scowling glare and vanished.

"Well," muttered Deedra, wondering what Mary Jane was doing in Rhonda's studio. Curious? After something damaging? Most women whose husbands had just been killed would have been distraught with grief. Many even required medical attention after the deaths because of the stress it can cause. Mary Jane was different though…tough. Perhaps she would never love anyone but herself. A strange woman without loyalties. If Deedra had to pick a killer from all the people at North Ledge, Mary Jane would be her choice.

Deedra hurried back to the church. She drove the 4-wheel rig to the far side of the church where it was shielded from view of the hotel, not wanting her actions observed. She placed her sleeping bag, fresh water, and food supplies in it, and after giving North Ledge a searching glance, backed onto the old stage road.

Mary Jane was suddenly at Rhonda's window, and watched as Deedra drove north toward the mixosaur site, then as if changing her mind, she turned and headed out the North San Juan Road. Mary Jane noted her progress, and Deedra knew that she was wondering where she was going and why. If Mary Jane was the one who took the map, at least she would know that Deedra wasn't going to the place of the gem discovery.

Deedra experienced a funny paranoid feeling that came with feeling her movements were being watched. She knew that Mary Jane was trying to guess where she was going. She gritted her teeth, not relaxing until she reached the ridge between North Ledge and the road to North San Juan. She cut west through sageland, over shale knolls, across an ancient river bed then up another hill, followed the ridge to a place where she could descend to the creek. It was a long round-about way, but she finally reached the adobe hut where she had left Brent. She parked the rig in a thicket, hoping it couldn't be seen by the men up on Mica Mountain, and then scurried behind trees and boulders.

"It's me, Brent," she said stepping into the hut.

There was only silence and for a moment her eyes didn't adjust to the sudden darkness.

The gun was aimed straight at her.

Brent smiled, a wan smile, and lowered his shaking hand.

Deedra saw that Brent was more alert than the previous day, though he was shivering and weak. "I brought you my sleeping bag. Get inside it, and I'll give you some hot coffee. I don't think I should give you any whiskey, though. It might be dangerous with that head injury."

When Brent had crawled into the sleeping bag, she asked, "How the hell are you feeling?" Her voice was husky with unexpressed emotion. She just wanted to crawl into the sleeping bag next to him and have the world go away. She might even be able to take advantage of him now, make him promise to marry her…soon.

"I'm going to make it, thanks to you. I thought I was a goner," Brent's eyes told her all she needed to know about those long hours in the funereal darkness of that mine shaft. Strong men were known to have gone mad in complete darkness without sound or hope. Deedra caught a glimpse of that awful time reflected in his dilated eyes.

Brent ate the food with certain gusto and she was relieved to see color return to his pale lips and cheeks.

"Gavin has the men up on Mica Mountain today. They're going to find that caved-in mine shaft, and then Gavin will call off the search. It's going to rain and cause travel to be next to impossible anyway."

"You told Gavin?"

"Yes." Deedra hesitated a moment. "Who tried to kill you?"

"I…I don't know. Someone hit me over the head when I walked around a large boulder. He had a bandanna over his face so I didn't even get a look at his eyes. It all happened really fast."

"Could it have been a woman?"

"I suppose so since everyone dresses in men's clothing. Whoever it was just hit me. I came to just as he pushed me down the mine tunnel in one of those old ore carts. The killer gave it a shove then walked back to the entrance. I heard the sound of a shot, and then the crack to timbers and earth falling. The ore cart rolled down the track out of the collapse area. Then it ran off the track and threw me several feet into another tunnel. The ore cart hit the side timbers and caused another collapse. It's buried in there somewhere. I was lucky to have been thrown free. I crawled along the tunnel to where you found me. I couldn't go any further, but did have plenty of air."

Brent paused, exhausted. After a moment of deep breathing he added, "I tried to fashion footholds in the side. It just can't be done without some sort of scaffold-

ing or a narrower shaft so you can lean against the
opposite wall while you climb."

Deedra nodded, visualizing Brent's efforts to get out
of that murky darkness.

"How did you happen to look there for me?" There
was a suspicion of tears in his gray eyes.

Deedra told him how she had searched for him, why
she had gone to the top of the mountain, and all the
while she prepared food for him for the next two days.
"Gavin wants to send you back to the city. He's afraid
the killer will find you here."

"Deedra, I'm not going."

"Nonsense. Remember, Brent, he who walks away,
lives to fight another day. Besides Gavin can't keep an
eye on you, and try to capture the killer, too."

"Yes, he can. He can use me for bait. After I gain
strength, then let the killer have enough rope. They always
go to extremes to cover up, you know. They'll do anything
necessary to keep their identity from being discovered."

"True," Deedra agreed.

"I think I can stay out of the killer's way long enough
to gain my strength. With the killer certain I'm dead, I
might prove useful later."

Deedra agreed, and then told him about finding
Gregg's gem deposit, and how she had drawn a map to
trap the killer, and how it had been stolen.

"It does give us leverage, though," Brent remarked.
"The murderer will have that map and sooner or later
will go to that place. That ought to indicate who it is."

"I think he's already checked it out, Brent. It would
have been easy during the search for you. He may
already know that he was set up."

"Hey, that puts you in more danger!"

Deedra busied herself filling the canteen with water, and putting writing materials close at hand so Brent would have something to while away the hours when he couldn't sleep.

"How valuable is that find?"

Deedra sighed. "I'd say it's very rich. I found gem aquamarines of good color, and perfectly terminated tourmalines, mixed with quartz crystals and muscovite mica. They're all used in industry even if the crystals aren't of jewel quality. Tourmaline is a rare crystal having pyroelectric and piezoelectric characteristics making it valuable in the manufacture of sophisticated electrical and electronic devices. It is also excellent in the manufacture of depth sounding apparatus, can accurately measure blast pressure both under water and in the air. It's also used in the optical industry because it is strongly dichroic. Beryl crystals are used as alloys to make certain fabrics, in making gyroscopes, and in the manufacture of space vehicles. So you can see that Gregg's find has immense possibilities."

Brent looked startled. "Gosh, Deedra, I wasn't aware that crystals were that important."

"They are minerals, of course, and radios, watches, and lots of other things can't be manufactured without garnet and quartz crystals. All minerals are valuable. Whatever is in that mine will make Gregg a wealthy man, and the killer might be aware of that. It's someone who recognizes the value of such minerals, though I don't think he knows the exact location yet."

"Deedra, don't go anywhere near it. In fact, be careful that you never go where the killer can sneak up on you."

"I'm cautious, Brent. Don't worry about me. I'm going to move into that empty store building next to the professors' place on Bridge Street. Now you just get well, and help me capture this murderer."

"Yeah," Brent murmured, fingering his head wound.

She checked the bandage and gave Brent two more aspirins.

WHEN DEEDRA PEERED OUT of the door of the hut she saw the men walking about on Mica Mountain. "I'll have to wait until they get out of sight on the other side of the ridge." She watched through binoculars from the shelter of a straggly tree next to the hut. The men were looking at the caved-in shaft and shaking their heads.

Far off lighting stabbed through heavy purple-black clouds, writhing and twisting through rain clouds causing strange light shadows across the sky. Resounding thunder boomed like far off cannon fire. The first of the rain splattered against the thick dust raising powdery puffs as it hit the thirsty earth. The air took on a fresh smell, clean and effervescent.

She knew the men on the mountain couldn't see her because she couldn't see them. After telling Brent she would return as soon as possible, ran to the rig. She had to hurry back before the rain made the road a sticky "gumbo." It took longer to reach the main North San Juan Road because the heavy rain had already washed away the tire tracks making it difficult to follow her own trail.

When she finally did reach the North San Juan Road, water sloshed across the road and once again she had to put the rig into "grandma" gear to keep from getting stuck. The men had returned to North Ledge and though no one was on the street, she knew that Gavin would be hoping that she wasn't stuck somewhere. She stopped in front of the old church to gather up her belongings and saw someone slip out the lean-to door and scurry toward Jackson Creek. The person ran in a crouched gait and she couldn't tell who it was.

FOURTEEN

THE DOOR SQUAWKED in protest as she pushed it open.

Suddenly the air was filled with the deadly rattle of a snake. Only by jumping sideways did she avoid the pit viper's sudden lunge.

She shuddered. Bile filled her mouth, nausea swept over her.

She watched the snake slither into the corner.

Released from the paralyzing fear, she killed the snake with a large rock she kept near the door, and then lurched out into the rain where she vomited the fear and revulsion away. Weakness from the trauma swiftly overtook her. She crept inside the building and huddled into several blankets and a heavy jacket. Tears slid down her face with the realization that the killer had struck out again.

That was the way Gavin found her.

"Deedra! Did you kill that damn rattler?" He stamped rainwater from his boots.

She nodded.

"Bite you?" Rain dripping from Gavin's jacket formed a pool of water around him.

"No."

Gavin breathed a sigh of relief and settled on the cold floor. "How's Brent?"

"Better. He has color in his face now, and his mind

is clear. There's no amnesia, and the pupils of his eyes are normal today. His pulse is strong and steady. If we can keep him quiet and warm he'll be okay."

"Did he see the killer?"

"No. I think it had to be a man, though. No woman could lift a man as big as Brent into that ore cart and get it started down those rusty tracks."

Gavin noted her understated tension, and went out to his vehicle, returning in a moment with a flask of whiskey. "Take a drink of this. It will drive thoughts of that old rattler from your mind." He threw another blanket around her shoulders then settled on the floor with his back against the wall. "Tell me about finding the rattler."

"I saw someone leave when I drove up, out through the lean-to. That means they put the snake in here to kill me, or at least get me away from North Ledge."

"Now, who knows how to handle rattlesnakes without getting bit?" Gavin's voice took on an iron edge.

"All the scientists would know and perhaps the others if they had studied survival techniques. Gregg and Frank. If someone watched it done on TV they could do it. Mary Jane probably knows how just from following Gregg and Alfred around in remote areas."

Gavin nodded. "That doesn't help. Strange. The puzzle gets more tangled all the time." Gavin shifted to a more comfortable position. "What motive is there for trying to kill Brent?"

"Because he was about to discover someone up there who didn't want to be seen, someone with a rifle, and perhaps Brent captured something in his photos that the killer doesn't want anyone to see."

Gavin agreed. "Yep, I think that's it, and it also takes our minds and thoughts off the other murders. Unless Brent saw something when he photographed the crime scene that was a clue there just doesn't seem to be a motive."

"I'm betting on the theory of diversion of attention. It takes our minds off the murders, clouds the real motives, and into a different realm of anxiety. This killer is very intelligent—the killings prove that. There are practically no clues. Anyone could have had the opportunity plus the fact that both Rhonda and Alfred were cousins, somehow connected. I think it's a psychological trick to confuse the motives."

"Derryck Evans could think of that. It's a clever tactic, all right."

Deedra sighed. "It's like that damn snake. Snakes automatically cause fear. If I got bit it would just be thought of as another accident, not a real killing. But it would get me out of North Ledge, reinforce the uneasiness and caution among the others here, and since I know where Gregg's find is, I wouldn't be here to hamper the killer's takeover."

Gavin missed Deedra's reference to Gregg's find, or for the moment was ignoring it. She wasn't sure which.

"Do you think they," Gavin gestured toward the hotel, "all know about applied psychology?"

Deedra shrugged. "They all graduated from college. A lot of college kids take basic psychology. Just whether they ever really used that knowledge, consciously used it, is doubtful. I just don't think they would think to use it. These events are more the process of a cold analytical mind. More like one of the scientists."

"How did you know that Gregg had made a find?"

Gavin's eyes were narrowed, sparking like a flint. It was as if he had suddenly realized the importance of her statement.

"From those drawings in his personal effects," Deedra still didn't say she had found it. "How did you find out about it?"

"The assay report was sent up here just after I arrived. Since Gregg is a suspect, we were alerted about it. Gregg found a valuable mine somewhere, though we're not certain it's up here."

"Has Gregg recorded the find?"

"Can't find any trace of it at the courthouse, so I don't think so. He hasn't left here in several weeks, just short trips to North San Juan for supplies and mail. I think he's waiting for the excitement about the mixosaur dig to be over, and for the scientists to clear out."

"They plan to move the fossils then?"

"Yes. They plan to move them to various museums. They'll mark the site of the dig, though. They're afraid another earthquake might move the block uplift again."

"Waiting until they leave sounds like what Gregg plans, especially with Mary Jane up here. He wouldn't want her to know anything about it."

Gavin questioned Deedra at length about Mary Jane and Gregg's marriage, though he didn't glean additional motive from their talk.

"What did the men say when they saw that caved-in mine shaft? Any suspicious actions?"

Gavin shook his head. "No, I didn't notice any. Either none of them is the killer or the killer is a damn good actor."

Deedra nodded. She hadn't expected any reaction. The killer had the time it took them to climb that mountain to prepare for the inevitable discovery of that caved-in mine shaft.

"They all agreed that there wasn't any other place he could have gone without a vehicle."

"While you were searching yesterday, Narkette had me search the rooms at the hotel." Deedra explained finding the tourmaline crystal in Rhonda's room.

"Yeah. Narkette told me he had you give them a look. He doesn't want to stir up their resentment, didn't want an official search."

"I didn't find any of Gregg's gems there either."

"Wait a minute, Deedra. Let's get something straight. You think Gregg's find is a gem mine instead of a copper mine?" Gavin was obviously puzzled.

Deedra experienced shock. "Copper? You mean it was an assay on copper?" Belatedly she realized that Gregg wouldn't have needed to test the gems since he obviously knew what they were. Did that mean that Gregg had discovered more than one mine or was it something from the mixosaur dig? She hadn't seen traces of the green of copper in the earth around the dig which proved nothing, of course. She hadn't been looking for copper and certainly wasn't an expert.

"Yes. Quite a rich deposit somewhere. Why did you think it was gems?"

Deedra explained about Gregg's drawings and how similar they were to the rich Himalaya pegmatite deposits of San Diego County.

"More motive than ever. Is there any way you can find out where copper can be found around here?" Gavin asked.

"I can try, but I honestly don't believe there's any

here. Are you sure that assay wasn't for some other part of the world? Have you asked Frank Shundo?"

"Yes. He was as surprised as you are."

They both knew Frank or the scientists were the only ones likely to have recognized copper minerals or know that Gregg had sent samples of copper off for analysis.

"Why did everyone ignore my questions about the copper samples when I asked earlier?" Deedra was miffed.

"We don't want anyone knowing we are looking for copper. Narkette doesn't think it has anything to do with the murders, and neither do I. He thinks Gregg found it on a search he did earlier this year in another state. I agree with that. I think he had the assay done here so the site there wouldn't be disclosed, and a run to establish claims started before whatever mining company he was working for had time to get located. No one we've interrogated has ever found copper up here."

"Do you still want me to look for traces of copper?"

"Yes. It can't hurt anything, and we can't overlook any kind of clue. I think it's farfetched to think copper samples have anything to do with Rhonda's murder, but with Alfred being a scientist it might. It's only important if Frank knows where a valuable copper mine is, one that Gregg has located, and Frank wants him arrested, out of the way."

Deedra snorted. "You know Frank wouldn't do a dirty trick like that!"

Gavin held up his hand. "Is copper ever found in the same general area as cinnabar?"

"I don't know. I'd have to look it up. It can be found in the same area with muscovite mica like that on Mica Mountain, and in porphyry rock. It's even possible that they discovered something at the dig, and that's why they're so reluctant to have visitors there."

Gavin nodded. "Narkette drove back to the city early this morning. He had an important case and was needed in court this afternoon. I don't think he worries about a missing news reporter."

Deedra smiled in a wry manner. "He better, this is an election year."

Gavin laughed.

"Gavin, when the D.A. searched, do you know if he found any books on mineralogy?"

"He didn't say, though there are quite a few in the lab. The professors brought them up here. Several shelves full, in fact."

"Anyone else?"

"Frank has several on various subjects about mining and things like that, and a few novels. Any reason why you're asking?"

Deedra frowned. "I just think it's strange that the killer left a mixosaur bone near Rhonda's body. If Rhonda had access to books on mineralogy, she might have been privy to some important information, might have tried to leave a clue."

"You've decided that old fossil bone is important?"

"What if Rhonda wrenched it out of the killer's hand, and he couldn't find it in the dark?"

Gavin scratched his head. "Well, no one's claimed that old bone, and if anyone knew it had been taken from the dig, they haven't admitted it. However, it would be just like Derryck to plant such a clue, and Shelley would know how distracting it would be in an investigation. And there's always the possibility that the bone was dropped there early in the evening and hasn't anything to do with Rhonda's murder."

"I'm going over to the professors' for a while. I'm supposed to be getting a story on that old reptile-fish. I need to observe those guys in their habitat anyway."

"Careful, Deedra. Remember, the killer seems to be after you. And from this latest act, I reckon he won't stop at anything."

Deedra recalled the buzzing snake with a shudder.

There was a sound of movement outside the church, and Gavin quickly strode to the door flinging it wide to find Frank with his fist raised ready to knock on the door. Frank flinched as if Gavin had suddenly hit him.

"Is Deedra here?" he stuttered.

"Come in, Frank."

Deedra remained where she was, huddled into the jackets. She was glad Gavin had gotten rid of the snake, but wanted to find out if Frank was the one who had put it there.

"I'll see you later, Deedra," Gavin gave her a warning glance.

"See ya, Gavin."

The door shut behind the sheriff shutting out the cold damp breeze left from the heavy downpour.

Frank looked at her and grinned. "Damn cold today. I thought you might need some cheering up after learning about Brent." He gave her a sympathetic look. If Frank was the one who had put the snake in here, Deedra was wrong about human nature. That kind of trick just wasn't in tune with the Frank she had known.

"Bad cave-in, Frank?"

"Yes. No way Brent could have survived it. And it's

impossible to get heavy equipment up there until it quits raining. They will have to bring it in by helicopter to get it up on the mountain."

"Frank, did Rhonda ever visit the scientists' quarters?"

Frank was obviously startled by her sudden change of subject, and sudden alertness lit his dark eyes. "Yes, I did see her there a time or two in the evening. Gregg and I saw here there while we were discussing mining. We used to talk in the Wells Fargo station after we found the professors eavesdropping behind my place. So after that we just moved across the street where it was more difficult for them to overhear us."

"Why would they want to eavesdrop?"

"Deedra, that mountain up there," Frank pointed to Mercury Mountain, "is loaded with cinnabar. Rich, very rich! I'm dragging my feet waiting for them to finish the dig. My company has all the claims recorded on that mountain. We just don't want a stampede up here. If those scientists get the idea there's going to be extensive mining up here, they'll stake out claims of their own and just cause nothing but trouble."

"Does Narkette know that?"

"No, I don't think so. I don't think it's occurred to him to question my company."

"Gregg knows how rich it is though?"

Frank nodded.

"And Gregg was aware that Rhonda visited the professors?"

Again Frank nodded.

"That fact, Frank, is going to keep you and Gregg from being charged with Rhonda's and Alfred's murders. I don't know how just yet, but it does show a connection with the scientists and makes that old fossil bone found beside her body mean something."

"How, Deedra? Anyone could have taken it from the dig or from the professors' place."

"I think it meant something special to Rhonda. Perhaps she left a clue to it in her writing. The fossil bone is supposed to be her way of revenge."

FIFTEEN

FRANK LOOKED SKEPTICAL. Deedra couldn't blame him. After all the suspicion and interrogation it was difficult for him to believe anything was going to help him or Gregg.

"Tell me what you know about everyone up here, Frank. Anything in their conversations that might have struck you as…ah…puzzling."

"I did think of something. Several things, in fact. I didn't tell the sheriff because he would probably think I was making it up to take the heat off myself."

"I doubt that."

"It's about that Shepley guy. He thought he was every woman's dream. You know the kind. Anyway, he tried to move in on Shelley Muldoon. He told her he knew she was an old flame of Gregg's, and knew she needed sympathy now that Gregg was interested in Valerie Penrose."

Deedra laughed. "What did Shelley do?"

Frank grinned. "Told him off and to mind his own business. He kept it up then Shelley kicked him where it really hurt when he tried to kiss her. Shelley could have killed Alfred right then she was so angry and disgusted with him."

"What was Alfred's reaction?"

Frank sobered. "He was the kind that held a grudge. After that he made scathing remarks about Shelley all the time. He was a real nasty character. Gregg got really furious over it, and told Shepley to keep his mouth shut. Actually, if Alfred had been killed right then instead of Rhonda, I'd have suspected Gregg did away with him. Alfred just couldn't take no for an answer. And he just couldn't seem to mind his own business. He snooped around Rhonda's studio. She was angry about it, and frightened, too, I think. He tried that with Mark Saylen. Mark beat him up in Boothill Alley after he found out that Alfred had searched his studio, had actually taken a manuscript without his permission." Frank paused, then grinned. "We thought Mark had taught him a lesson in how to mind his own business. It didn't seem to help though, because Alfred was just as snoopy as ever only he hated Mark after that. Alfred had the gall of a crocodile to take one of Mark's manuscripts, then to quote from it! That's the kind of guy he was though, and it's not really surprising that he ended up getting killed."

"Mark beat up Alfred?

"Yes. I didn't tell the sheriff. I don't like to tattle, and I sure didn't want it to look as if I was pointing fingers to take the heat off myself. Besides, I wasn't the only one who knew about it, and I figured someone else might tell Gavin."

Deedra nodded, remembering that Frank never really passed judgment on others, and never tattled. She recalled the day at school when he had taken the punishment for something he hadn't done rather than tattle on a friend.

"What did Alfred do after Mark beat him up?"

Frank shook his head. "You know how those guys are! Alfred acted scared of Mark, though once in awhile he would make a remark about his writing. Alfred could always dish it out, but never was able to take it. No backbone, all jellyfish!"

Deedra laughed. It was such an adequate description of Alfred Shepley's character. No one could have described him better. Deedra felt sympathy for Mark and Shelley. She detested people who deliberately butted into things that were none of their business, creating trouble when none had existed earlier.

"That gives Mark and Shelley motives to kill Alfred."

"I doubt Shelley killed him, though she really hated him," Frank sighed.

Deedra waited a moment to give importance to her next suggestion. "Frank, do you suppose someone took the opportunity to get rid of Alfred at a time when everyone would think the murders are connected?"

"I've thought of that," Frank replied. "It's possible, but doesn't really explain why the murderer tried to kill you."

"I think the killer saw me warn you not to say the knife that killed Alfred was yours. It's evident that he tried to implicate you. He's hoping Gavin will learn about the knife. Then when the killer searched me, he found gems from Gregg's find."

"You have gems?" Frank's eyes took on an excited glint.

Deedra learned what she had wanted to know. Frank hadn't asked, "You found Gregg's discovery?"

"Yes. I don't know why the killer took them, only that it means he or she could recognize them, didn't want them found on my dead body." Deedra shifted to a more comfortable position. "Is there any copper deposits up here? There were copper formulas for several copper minerals with Gregg's drawings. Gavin asked me to look for signs of copper since Gregg sent in for an assay on some very rich copper. We all think it's from some other place, but Gavin can't overlook anything. How it could have anything to do with Rhonda's murder is beyond me."

"I've really looked up here, Deedra, and haven't found any signs of copper. I'm sure if you ask Gregg he'll tell you that sample is from Montana where he did some prospecting earlier this year for Anaconda Copper. That's not saying there isn't any in that old porphyry around the mixosaur dig. They never let me close enough to it to find out for sure."

"It's possible though?"

"Well, anything is possible. I just don't believe there's any copper up here, but I've no idea what the block uplift has done. Just the fact that they found the mixosaur proves that anything is possible."

"Did you know that Rhonda and Alfred were cousins?"

Frank was startled. "That certainly explains a lot of things. And why Mary Jane and Alfred seemed friendly with Rhonda."

Suddenly Deedra recalled Derryck's presence in Mary Jane's house after they found Alfred's body. It seemed then as if they were more than mere acquaintances. Did Mary Jane have something going with Derryck? That might give Derryck a motive. Strange, now that she thought about it, Mary Jane was Gregg's ex-wife, here with her new husband, and in the same remote area with her husband's cousin. Then suddenly both cousins were murdered. Was that only coincidence? Gregg and Alfred had adequate reasons for being in North Ledge, but Mary Jane's and Rhonda's presence were vague. When she recruited the artists, had Rhonda known that Alfred and Mary Jane were here?

"Do you think the scientists overheard you tell Gregg about Mercury Mountain? I mean how rich it is in cinnabar?"

"No. I told him one day when he and I hiked Mercury Mountain. We didn't go near the place where the richest deposit is. It was other things they overheard, like talk about Mary Jane and things like that. I guess that's how they knew Gregg had been married to Mary Jane because Gregg didn't tell them. It made Alfred furious when he learned that the men at the dig all knew that Mary Jane had been Gregg's wife first. He hated that, and whenever he got out of line, one of the professors would remind him of it. It kept old Alfred fuming most of the time."

"Didn't the professors like Alfred?"

"They only tolerated him." Frank gave her a smile. "They hated having him around. He wasn't invited here by them, you know. He just showed up one day with permission from the state. He does have a degree in paleontology, or did have, I should say. They couldn't keep him away."

Deedra noted that Frank still used the present tense, as if Alfred was still alive, another indication that he was not the killer.

"Then Alfred managed to get some sort of credential which the professors didn't have, and that caused trouble. John Drake told me that they had a hell of a fight up at the dig. Steven Robbins hit Alfred. I gathered Alfred had nerve enough to tell Robbins that he didn't know what he was talking about. That was pure jealousy on Alfred's part though, and really stupid because after that they treated him as if he didn't have any sense."

"Ah, Frank, you have just opened a can of worms. The professors have all insisted that everything was fine up at the dig. That means they lied. Why?"

"You know how touchy scientists are when they have discovered something as important as the mixosaur quarry. It just means they didn't want any delays in their work."

"Perhaps." Deedra felt that it was an excellent opportunity to rid themselves of Alfred Shepley's unwanted interference. That fact couldn't be ignored. It didn't explain Rhonda's murder though. There was the possibility that Mary Jane had killed both her husband and Rhonda which seemed to make more sense than anything else.

"Why did Mary Jane go up to the dig all the time?"

Frank glanced at her. "You know the answer to that. Gregg was up there. Then after he and Valerie Penrose became an item, she had to continue to go up there just to prove that Gregg wasn't the reason."

Deedra nodded. "Is she trying to get Gregg back?"

Frank ran a hand through his dark hair. "No, I don't think so. From what Gregg said, it was more that she was trying to get him use his influence to get Alfred a better position, something like that. Perhaps a teaching post at another university. Gregg told me she used threats which he ignored. He did say it made things miserable at the dig with her always there. Whenever he could, Gregg would just take off where Mary Jane couldn't follow."

"Did Mary Jane try?"

"No. After he would leave she'd get sullen and grouchy at Alfred about everything. Steven told me that."

"Have you had a lot of conversations with the professors?"

"Yeah, before all this happened. I'd go over to the lab once in awhile, and sometimes we'd get together for card games at night. Whenever anyone went into town they brought back beer so we would all get together then."

"Was Alfred included?"

Frank shook his head. "No. That's why we went to the professors' place. It was off limits to Alfred. He knew better than to ask."

Deedra wanted to tell Frank that Brent was alive and only knew it would endanger Frank, and if by remote chance he was the killer, endanger Gregg. Here she was, trusting Frank and not trusting him. Yet it was the only thing to do at the moment.

"I saw Derryck sneaking out of the scientists' place the other day, Frank. Any reason he would want to get in there?" Deedra wondered if Derryck had been the one who had taken the fossil bone.

"That doesn't surprise me. He sneaks in every place and takes pictures of rooms, then super-imposes unreal creatures on them. It made Mark mad as hell one day when he discovered Derryck had turned his studio into one of his fantasy painting settings. Another thing. Alfred liked porno, and would go to Rhonda's place every chance he got to read that trash she wrote."

The thought that Derryck could be the killer slipped into her mind. Perhaps Gavin's suspicions were correct. "Derryck might have a motive for wanting Rhonda and Alfred dead. As Gavin said, he might have acted out his fantasies. Maybe he wanted a cut in the porn market. Alfred's death was inevitable. Alfred probably saw the killer and made the mistake of letting the killer know it."

"You know," Frank drawled, "Rhonda might have been killed by mistake. The killer might have thought she was someone else. Rhonda was afraid of the dark. It's strange that she was in that alley alone."

"Perhaps she wasn't alone. Maybe she met the killer there. She had to have a market for that porn stuff, and someone might have been in partnership with her. It's certain that she had to have a contact of some sort."

Frank nodded agreement. "She drove off somewhere several weeks ago with a stack of manuscripts. I think she met someone along the road somewhere." He gave her an inquisitive look. "How did you know that Rhonda and Alfred were cousins?"

"Gavin told me. He has dossiers on everyone. I don't think Mary Jane knows that Gavin knows that fact, though."

"Does Gavin think I killed Rhonda?"

Deedra noted that Frank didn't say "and Alfred." "No. He thinks you're too smart to leave a knife with Gregg's initials on it in a woman's back."

Frank flinched. "No, I'd never set Gregg up like that."

Again Deedra noted that he didn't say he wouldn't kill Alfred, but the fact that he had returned from the direction of Mercury Mountain suggested that he wasn't aware that Alfred lurked in the dark alley. He did leave his abode again and could have slipped into Boothill Alley then sneaked around to Dead Man's Alley. Frank could probably kill if given motive enough.

They discussed motives for everyone without any

conclusions. It was difficult for Deedra to pretend grief for Brent when all the while she knew he was alive. Frank stayed a long time. He had received so much rejection that it seemed to give him a sense of security to have someone he trusted to talk to, to accept him. Deedra just wished she could confide about Brent and the false map she had drawn, tell him that someone had already stolen it. It would help she and Gavin if they could depend on Frank's help.

Later, when the rain slacked off leaving huge mucky puddles though freshly cleansed air, Deedra limped up the road. Instead of crossing Stagecoach Bridge, she went across the bridge on Front Street leading to the professors' quarters. She had decided to wait until the next day to move next door to them.

She was about to knock when she heard arguing going on within. The voices were low-pitched, but had that dangerous threatening tone.

Deedra wasn't the eavesdropping type, but since she was looking for a killer, she pushed scruples aside and strained to hear the words.

SIXTEEN

"IT WAS HERE UNTIL Rhonda's murder, I tell you! That damn Alfred Shepley took it, I'm certain of it!" Deedra recognized Dr. Von Kraus' hiss.

"It wasn't in Shepley's house. I searched, and then the District Attorney went all through it," Steven Robbins answered.

"It couldn't have just walked out of here!" Von Kraus replied in a voice dripping with sarcasm.

"Someone else could have taken it, you know," Robbins replied.

"Who else knew of its value?" scoffed Von Kraus. "Gregg wasn't even there when I found it, but Alfred was."

"I think Rhonda took it."

"And the killer took it from her?" John Drake suggested. "She certainly sneaked around here often enough."

"How did the killer know she had it?" Von Kraus sputtered.

"Maybe Rhonda told him. She was a very devious person, always creating problems. It might even have been you, Kurt. You might have met her in the alley, and when she didn't hand it over you killed her."

"I certainly wouldn't have removed it from the bone, Robbins, and you know it. That's what gave it value," Kurt hissed.

"Those young people at the hotel wouldn't realize that. They aren't even interested in the dig," John Drake pointed out. "But a big gold nugget like that would be a temptation to anyone."

"Unless someone told them, they didn't even know that it existed," Von Kraus insisted.

"Alfred could have told Mary Jane or Rhonda," Steven Robbins replied.

"But now the fossil has no value," Von Kraus moaned.

Deedra got the impression he was so enraged that he might jump up and down and stamp his feet.

"The find was unique, no doubt about that," Steven replied. "'We'll just have to be on the watch, and see if anyone happens to find a gold nugget."

"I've never seen anything like that in a fossil bone before. It makes it the most interesting find of the century. I'm not going to let someone else steal it from me!" Von Kraus sounded determined…and threatening.

"Kurt, we've searched and searched for it. It just isn't anywhere in this shack."

"You should have left it up at the dig anyway," Robbins said in disgust. "If you had left it there, no one would have taken it. We always made certain that Shepley left first and no one else knew anything about it. Not even that nitwit wife of his."

"Not unless he told her," Von Kraus reminded in his special, sarcastic way.

"I'm sure he didn't. He planned to use that knowledge to get a teaching position in some university. He didn't want Mary Jane to know about it yet," Steven replied.

"You don't think he told her?" Kurt sounded mollified.

Deedra felt that she had eavesdropped long enough.

Dusk had settled. Long shadows crept across the road. Stillness had descended on North Ledge, a haunting quiet that caused Deedra an unaccountable shiver. The age-old superstition that someone had just walked over her grave flashed into her mind. She shook her head to rid such imaginings, and then knocked on the door.

For an eon of time there was a heavy silence, then heavy footsteps, and then Dr. John Drake stood in the doorway with an inquiring look on his face. When he saw her, his eyes lit up and he gestured her in with, "So you've come to get that big story on the mixosaur, have you?"

Deedra nodded. "Yes. Do you mind?"

Dr. Drake stood aside and she entered the brightly lighted lab. Everywhere there were the tools and impediments of their endeavors.

"You do have a complete lab here! Gavin told me that you did, but I didn't think it was quite this…ah… modern."

John Drake smiled his best and most charming smile, all the while Deedra was wondering if they knew or suspected that she had overheard their conversation.

"Not at all unusual when scientists are in the field for any length of time. It saves time and money when cities are so far away. We generate our own electricity to run it. I'll show you the generator later. I'll let you see what we have accomplished this far."

Drake went into a lengthy conversation about carbon 14 dating of the fossil bones, and about how they had determined that it was a mixosaur rather than a simple ichthyosaur, and what they had learned from the block uplift.

"Where do you think the mixosaur originated?" she asked.

"Probably over in ancient Lake Lahonton where the ichthyosaurs were found. It's in an almost direct line from that site, and could easily have been displaced by gradual uplifting. Another big earthquake could ruin it for us, and that's why we're moving the fossils to museums and universities. This is the only find of its kind in this part of the world. Therefore its value to the scientific world is inestimable."

Von Kraus was suspicious of her. She could feel the hostility in his gaze, knew he resented her knowing anything about what they were doing.

They talked on about the mixosaur description, and Deedra told of her visit to the site near Gabbs, Nevada. "You found the same type ammonites and trilobites as in Nevada?"

"Yes. The geology is similar in the block uplift itself, not native to the rest of the strata in this area. It looks as if it moved up with the molten movement of some of the gold found in this area. Perhaps an earthquake moved it into a fissure that otherwise would have been filled with metal ore. It will take more study and comparison with the Nevada site to establish those theories beyond a doubt."

Dr. Drake went on explaining about the scientific paraphernalia and what the tests were and how many they had conducted, which tests had proved out, and which hadn't. It was all a very slow and exact study. Deedra knew then that it was going to take them all summer, or perhaps even into the following year to complete the excavation of the quarry and make the necessary tests.

Would Frank's mining company wait that long? She

doubted it. They would probably set up mining operations in late summer complete with guards. Then Mercury Mountain would be posted and the professors' presence barely tolerated.

Deedra noted two complete sets of Dana's System of Mineralogy, a reference on geology and paleontology. Fossil bones were spread out, tagged with their description and location in the mixosaur skeleton. Anyone visiting there could take one if unobserved.

She was surprised to find that it was completely dark outside when she left, knowing there was no chance to move that night. She regretted not having done it earlier in the day. Her eyes had trouble adjusting when she stepped from the brightly lit lab, and was apprehensive at being alone in the dark. Later, she wondered why she hadn't gone to Gavin's or Gregg's place.

With a thumping heart, she crossed the bridge and started the trek up to the old church. It now seemed far away, a dark blob against the night sky. She kept to the center of the road knowing that rattlesnakes were out looking for prey at that time of night, though perhaps the rain had caused them to den early. Her nerves couldn't stand another encounter with one of those buzzing reptiles.

There was a haunting stillness, an unquiet silence as if the ghosts of the old town were flitting about. She glanced over her shoulder every few minutes, her arm aching in recollection. She was half-way to the church when she intuitively sensed that she was being followed. The hair on the nape of her neck tingled.

She halted…listening. Only night birds off near Jackson Creek and the hum of locusts pierced the silence, and then a mournful howl of a coyote up on Mica Mountain.

The stalker was between her and North Ledge.

She limped forward, glancing over her shoulder. Though she didn't see anyone, she knew someone followed. With quick movements that she hoped would startle the stalker, she ran into the sage at the base of Mercury Mountain, across from the old church, hoping to circle around to North Ledge.

Crashing noises broke the uneasy silence as the stalker chased her. There was a sudden muttered groan followed by silence.

She huddled next to the trunk of a scrub pine, waiting, her heart fluttering. She couldn't hope to outrun the killer with her sprained ankle. Would he try to sneak up on her or go back to North Ledge? She hoped the groan had meant that he was hurt enough to give up the pursuit. Then she realized that he might eventually go to the church and wait for her there.

Far off on Mica Mountain, the coyote howled away at the moon. Then another coyote took up the call, and soon the valley was filled with their haunting cries.

Birds took up renewed twittering along Jackson Creek as if distracted in their night roosts. Close to Deedra at the foot of Mercury Mountain there were no cricket sounds, no nocturnal movements of creatures on their nightly treks. Their very silence was a warning of danger.

Standing there in the shadow of the scrub pine, Deedra realized that if she moved, if she attracted attention by the slightest noise, it could very possibly cause her death.

SEVENTEEN

It TURNED COLD. Straggly mists began to rise from the damp ground. A strong wind blew up the canyon riffling her short curls. She soon became chilled through and through. She clenched her teeth to keep them from chattering which caused her jaws to ache. The killer would count on her getting cold enough to seek shelter. She reckoned her only chance was to climb Mercury Mountain, though hesitated to do that in the dark. Not only were there rattlers, her ankle was at risk. If she sprained it again, she would be at the killer's mercy. Her chattering teeth made a clicking sound in her head that she feared the killer could hear.

The night remained undisturbed, but the fact that the creatures were quiet told her something had alarmed them. She knew better than to move and give her location away. After an endless stretch of time she heard furtive movements in the brush near the road.

At first she thought the noise was created by the stalker. In a few minutes someone stood quite close to her and created a dark blob in the night sky. She held her breath in an attempt to remain quiet.

Eventually whoever it was ambled off into the darkness.

The sudden release of tension relaxed muscles and her shoulders sagged. She felt a need to run and scream,

and ached for warmth knowing that she was risking hy-
pothermia if she stayed where she was.

Luckily before she had a chance to make a move, the
killer suddenly appeared on the knoll above her. He was
a furtive shadow silhouetted against the night sky. The
stalker was within yards of her, though he didn't see her
through the sheltering fringe of the scrub pine. Deedra
couldn't identify the man who was dressed in bulky
clothes and wore a bandanna over his face. He
crouched on the knoll, waiting, watching, like a bandit
of the Old West.

Deedra didn't dare even shift her weight.

The night went on and on with no moon. Only occasionally did stars peek between rain-laden clouds that
rode the south wind. Still the killer crouched on the hill,
waiting and watching. The coyotes continued their wails
of frustration, howling and yapping mournful tunes.

Deedra could see that their cries bothered the killer
who moved restlessly each time the haunting coyotes'
howls echoed up and down the valley. She hoped those
uncanny yelps would eventually drive the killer to
shelter. And finally they did. After a prolonged serenade,
the man grunted and strode off through the sage toward
the old church.

Deedra shuddered.

When the crashing noises finally faded away, she
began circling around toward North Ledge, planning to
seek shelter under the bridge and wait for the killer to cross
over so she could identify him. It took longer to reach the
bridge than she had expected. A sudden flash of lightning
followed by a roll of thunder promised more rain.

She stumbled and sprained her ankle again causing

flashes of light in front of her eyes. This slowed her progress to a painful foot dragging. Constant shivering from the cold and exhaustion nearly overcame her determination to reach the bridge. Finally she limped to the bridge, dropped down onto the bank beside it on one foot.

The water gave off an icy chill increasing her discomfort. She was dreadfully weary, and after a few minutes of indecision, realized that the killer wouldn't return to North Ledge that way, would circle around to prevent the risk of being seen.

She took a deep breath, then clambered up the bank, and scurried to Gavin's place.

"Gavin! Gavin! Open up. Let me in!"

Deedra did not see the dark shadow that melded into the murkiness of Dead Man's Alley.

There was a scrambling noise from within, and the door squeaked open. "What the hell are you doing wandering around at this time of night, Deedra?" Gavin growled.

"Let me in, Gavin. I'm nearly frozen to death!"

Once she was inside, Gavin gave her a drink from his whiskey flask then put a blanket around her shoulders. "Now, tell me what this is all about!" Gavin was obviously irritated.

Deedra almost cried at his lack of sympathy. She hadn't, after all, asked to come up here, Gavin had requested it.

Quickly, she told him what happened. Gavin hurried to the church, traversing along Jackson Creek, hoping to take the killer by surprise. The church was empty and he returned in a fit of frustration.

"No one there, probably heard you call me, and is

back where he belongs now. No way of telling who it was." Gavin took several strides around the room. "Was there anything familiar about him?"

"No. The only thing I am sure of is that it was a man, moved in a masculine way, taller than Shelley or Mary Jane."

Gavin nodded. "You said the coyotes made him uneasy? That sounds more like a woman." Gavin took another stride around the room then cleared his throat. "There are eight men here. Any of them could have been out there. Especially if they knew you were in the scientists' place until dark. He would know that you would be walking up that old road alone."

Deedra nodded, recalling how dark it had been when she left the lab, how the locusts had stopped chirping as if in warning, how haunting it had been, and shook off another shudder. "Gavin, have you got anything to eat? I haven't eaten since yesterday morning."

Gavin gave her crackers and canned sardines which she washed down with water drawn from the old well earlier in the evening.

In the security of Gavin's presence, she fell into a deep sleep from which she didn't wake until late afternoon. Gavin hadn't told anyone where she was, and watched while Frank had searched all morning for her. Gavin was hoping the killer would give himself away, but the scientists had gone off to the dig, and the young people were occupied with their creative pursuits. Only Frank seemed disturbed by her absence.

Gavin had watched Frank go into the church, search around it, and then up and down Jackson Creek. He returned to the old bridge, and then walked slowly up the stage road evidently following her foot-prints. He continued following the prints, found where she had left the road, and began to search on the slopes of Mercury Mountain. He lost Deedra's trail, retraced his footsteps, and went down to the road again. After a time he checked out the footprints again.

Gavin was convinced that Frank had not been the one to stalk Deedra. He would have only given it a cursory search and left. Frank was genuinely puzzled. No one else seemed to realize that she was missing.

Later, Deedra asked Gavin, "Do you think Frank suspects that Brent was deliberately done away with?"

"Probably. Frank's no fool. That cave-in might have looked deliberate to him, and no doubt he has his own idea about the identity of the culprit."

Deedra nodded. "Do you want me to just turn up, or say that someone followed me last night and I took refuge here?"

"Go out the back door and hide in the livery stable until you can sneak over to see how Brent is doing. I don't have a chance to check on him right now. Just get back here before dark."

Cold fear caused perspiration to sprout on her forehead. Urgency to get to Brent right away whether anyone saw her or not was a temptation she had to curb. She had to wait, and waiting was not one of the things Deedra did without frustration. She was a person of action, not inaction, and always fumed and fussed at un-necessary delays. She kept telling herself that Brent was all right, but doubt plagued her, and she was only comforted in the knowledge that she had given him her sleeping bag and that he probably hadn't been cold last night. He also had a gun and was not afraid to shoot it.

Deedra was unaware that Frank knocked on Gavin's door just seconds after Deedra had slipped into the livery stable.

"I can't find her, Gavin. Where do you think she went?"

"Probably out hiking and that ankle gave her trouble. She went up to the professors' last night after you left her. Let's take a ride up to the dig, and see what they have to say about it."

"Right."

Deedra, peering through a crack in the old livery stable wall, saw Frank and Gavin roar across Stage-coach Bridge in Gavin's rig.

She glanced toward the old hotel noting that Shelley was on the balcony, and Zach Johnson was standing at his window. When the sound of the engine died away, they both turned away, presumably to return to their creative projects.

She watched another few minutes, and there was no further activity. She was about to leave when Mary Jane crossed Frontier Street and entered the hotel.

Deedra couldn't believe her good luck at having Mary Jane away from her living quarters where she wouldn't see her crossing Boothill Ridge.

She crawled through a hole in the far wall, the place where the killer had dropped all the knives, then limped along Jackson Creek until she reached the place where the creek circled back toward North Ledge, scrambled up Boothill Ridge, then hobbled along the barren slope hoping no one would notice.

Finally she was out of sight. Without fear she made

better progress. It wasn't far when she walked directly to the adobe hut, instead of circling around to get there.

When she got close to the hut she called out, "Brent, it's me."

There was no answer.

When she opened the door, she found the hut empty. Even the sleeping bag and supplies she had provided were gone. There was no sign that Brent had ever been there.

It was as if, Deedra thought wildly, she had dreamed it all…that Brent was still trapped in that old mine shaft!

EIGHTEEN

THERE WAS A STEALTHY noise behind her.

Deedra screamed.

"For gosh sakes, Deedra, quit screaming!" Brent hissed in her ear.

Deedra sagged to the floor, her knees suddenly giving way. "Don't you ever do that to me again!"

Brent leaned against the door of the hut. "What's the matter?"

"What the hell are you doing out of bed?" Deedra spat out. "You know you aren't supposed to walk around when you've got a head wound, possibly a concussion." She was furious at finding Brent walking around when she had been so worried about him.

"Take it easy, Deedra. I had to move out of here. Someone was out there during the night. I had to shoot at him to scare him away. Soon as it got light, I moved my gear out of here so I wouldn't be here if he came back."

"Where did you move? Into that old mine shaft?"

"No, I'll never go into an old mine shaft again! Anyway, the killer would look there right away. There's a sort of shelter in the cliff right up there," Brent gestured to a place above the hut. "It can't be seen from here, and I took a branch and wiped out all my footprints after I carried everything up there. Been waiting for him to return to see who it is."

"That's really strange. The killer followed me last night after I left the professors. I had to spend the night hiding out on Mercury Mountain. He couldn't have been two places at once."

Brent slumped against the wall. "Who could it have been then?"

"Are you certain it was a man?" Deedra noted the perspiration of weakness on Brent's forehead.

"No. I couldn't see who it was."

"What time was that?"

"Toward morning, not yet light, though."

"Hmm. Could have been the killer. I heard him head for that old church. He probably followed Jackson Creek and up over the ridge so he could enter town from the opposite direction. You must have scared him to death shooting like that. He won't know it's you because he knew you didn't have a gun when he shut you up in that tunnel. My guess is that he'll think it's an old miner staying in this hut."

"I hope you're right. I'm not going to be in this hut when he returns tonight."

"He won't come back at night and take a chance on getting shot. You'll be wise to hole up here instead of where anyone can find you, shoot you from the ridge. In this hut they can't see you, and there's only one door."

Brent nodded, slightly embarrassed at having over-looked that fact.

They moved his gear back into the hut. After the last trip, Brent slouched to the floor exhausted. Deedra shook her head in exasperation. Brent had taken such a chance. What if he had passed out while moving his things to that shelter?

She found several boards to use to bar the door. Even if Brent was asleep it would cause noise if someone tried to get in, giving him time to get the gun.

After Brent was huddled into the sleeping bag again and she made certain he had food and water she told him she had to go. "I can't wander around in the dark again tonight!"

"Okay, just be careful. Scream if anyone follows. Over there in that old ghost town noises like that echo against those old buildings."

"Yep. You need anything before I go?"

"Not for a day or two, then I'll run out of food again." Deedra nodded.

She climbed the cliff behind the hut and followed the ridge as it wended to the north so she would enter town from the old North San Juan Road.

The men had not yet returned from the dig, and she was about to search the lab when she noted Derryck and Mark Saylen watching her, curiosity plain on their faces. It was obvious that they were wondering why she was walking around with that sprained ankle.

"Darn," she muttered, knowing that another opportunity to search the lab was lost.

She was standing on the church steps when Gavin, Frank, and the professors drove in from the dig. Gavin whirled his vehicle and drove right up to the church steps.

"Where have you been, Deedra?" Frank jumped out even before Gavin could get the rig stopped.

Gregg sat beside Gavin, watching her with curiosity. Did Gregg resent her presence in North Ledge? He

avoided her, didn't seem to want to talk. Even now, he
didn't join in Frank's relieved excitement.

"I really wasn't missing, Frank. Just hiding out."

"You mean?" Frank nodded toward Mercury Mountain.

"Yeah, the killer followed me from the professors'
place and I had to hide out. Sorry I caused you to worry."

"I'm just glad he didn't kill you!" Frank wiped his
forehead with the back of his hand.

"You two come to my place. We need to talk. Then
Frank, you help Deedra move into that empty building
next to the professors. She isn't going to stay out here
away from the rest of us anymore."

They climbed into Gavin's rig and drove to the place
the sheriff called home.

Gavin began supper preparations. "We can't be overheard here easily with that battery radio on. Talk low."

Frank nodded, happy to be included after all the rejection he had received.

Deedra's appetite returned and reflected on how
mountain air made food taste better.

"Did you get a chance to check on Brent?"

She nodded.

"Brent? Is Brent alive?" Frank was genuinely surprised.

"Yes. Deedra winched him out of that old mine shaft
before it collapsed. Now, Frank, I'm telling you this in
strictest confidence. If the killer realizes that Brent is
alive, he'll try to kill him again. We can't let that happen.
We have to hide Brent until he's well enough to walk
around." Gavin was giving Frank the test to find out if
he was the murderer. If Frank was the killer, he would
immediately and "accidentally" let the others know so

that any future attempt on his life would not eliminate any of the others as suspects.

Deedra covertly watched Frank. There was no indication that Brent's being alive bothered him. On the contrary, he seemed relieved. Though they believed Frank innocent, they dared not let him know where Brent was hiding.

"Brent was all right, you said?" Gavin asked again.

"Yes, still alive and he has food and water for several days."

Gavin nodded, saluting Deedra with a flash of his gray eyes. Deedra knew how to bait traps for killers. Newsmen called it know-how, law officers called it justice. If Frank was the killer, he would prepare an alibi. If he was innocent, he would not divulge this information until the sheriff gave him permission to do so. Gavin and Deedra would watch and wait.

It was at that moment that Deedra realized that the person who took her map had already had the opportunity to look where she had indicated on her map while searching for Brent. And now the killer realized that the map had been a trick. That explained last night's attempt on her life.

"Gavin, let's go over those clues again. Everyone had the opportunity to kill Rhonda and Alfred, but who had the opportunity to kill me last night?"

"Everyone here. Anyone could have been aware of the time you left the professors. They have strong lights in that lab and when the door is open, it throws a long beam. You stood right in the light. There's just no way to check on who it was. Everyone has to use outdoor plumbing. No one pays any attention, it's such a usual thing."

"With that back door of the lab oiled so that it doesn't squeak, one of those professors could have been out all night and the others wouldn't have even known of it," Deedra mused.

Gavin nodded. "They probably all sleep soundly at night, physically tired from work at the dig. That's strenuous work. As long as they're all there in the morning, they wouldn't know that anyone left during the night or not. Even if they heard someone they would just think it was a call of nature."

"Did you know that the back door of the hotel doesn't squeak either?" Frank remarked.

The sheriff nodded.

"The only real clue is those damn knives. There's something about the initials on that knife that bothers me," Deedra remarked. "Gavin, do you have a photo of that knife?"

"Yeah," Gavin rummaged around in his books and papers and produced a police photo of the knife that had killed Rhonda.

"That doesn't look like the way Gregg writes, Frank."

"No, it isn't. Gavin has a sample of his handwriting."

Deedra studied the photo again. Except for the initials, there was nothing to tell it from all the other knives, nothing to really implicate Gregg. She didn't say anything about Frank's knife being the one that had killed Alfred. It had been different only by a deep scratch in the hilt that Frank recognized.

"Now, we have to remember that Alfred Shepley probably saw the killer go into the alley about the time Rhonda was killed. Mary Jane was vague about the time, which may or may not mean she was in the place at that time. Alfred evidently recognized the killer and was foolish enough to let him know it."

"Alfred was the blackmailing type," Deedra suggested.

Gavin nodded. "Yes, I think that's what happened. I think Alfred pressured the killer, causing his own murder. Of course, there's always the possibility that Mary Jane did away with him for the insurance, an opportune time to cause us to believe the killer had struck again." He sighed. "In that case, we would have two murderers."

Deedra told the sheriff what she had overheard outside the scientists' lab. "They think Alfred took something Dr. Von Kraus found at the dig." Deedra saw Frank give a start of surprise and wondered if Gavin noticed.

"What the hell could they have discovered up there except those old fossil bones?" Gavin looked from Deedra to Frank and back again.

"A large gold nugget. Evidently it was embedded in that fossil bone you found beside Rhonda's body. Von Kraus is really upset that it has disappeared. I'd hate to be on his drop-dead list."

"Did they have any explanation why it was beside Rhonda's body?" Gavin's eyes had taken on a steely glint.

"They think Rhonda stole it, and the killer took the gold nugget. Von Kraus claims it ruins its scientific value. Only the scientists would care that it remained intact. Anyone else would just want the nugget."

"Hmm…that would explain why the bone was discarded," Gavin replied. "The thing is that none of them has reported this theft to me or the D.A." He slammed a fist on the plank desk. "I had the notion they were holding out on me."

"You'd probably better pretend that you don't know anything about it," Deedra advised. "You said something about Mary Jane inheriting Alfred's insurance? A big policy?"

"Yep," he sighed, "$100,000. That fact takes a lot of heat off Gregg. Have you had a chance to talk to him?"

"Not since the day I arrived. He spends his spare time with Valerie." Deedra wondered if Gregg was really avoiding her or if he just didn't want to tell her about the gem mine knowing that she had seen the drawings. He knew she would have questions about them.

Frank was leaning against the wall and suddenly tensed. His eyes took on a fierce glitter. He jerked the door open.

There was the sound of running footsteps fading into the darkness of Dead Man's Alley.

"Damn!" Frank muttered.

Gavin strode outside and turned on his vehicle lights. It illuminated an empty street. Dead Man's Alley was as ghostly as its name. There was no use searching since the eavesdropper would be safe in his abode by the time they could even begin to look.

"Gavin, Frank told me that he and Gregg were forced to spend the evenings over at Gregg's because they caught the professors eavesdropping."

Gavin showed surprise. "Is that right?"

Frank nodded.

"Which ones?"

"Von Kraus for sure. I think Steven Robbins was the other one, though I couldn't really see who it was. Just the general build of the man, and it seemed to me that it was Steven Robbins."

Deedra had a sudden thought. "Gavin, have you ever noticed how much Steven and Derryck look alike when their backs are turned? They're both tall and slender and hold their shoulders in a similar manner." She turned to Frank. "Could it have been Derryck?"

Frank frowned. "I suppose, though I really thought it was Steven Robbins. Derryck wasn't all that interested in our talk about mining and geology."

"I asked you earlier, Frank. What kind of minerals are up on Quartz and Feather mountains?" Gavin sounded angry.

"Let me think," Frank paused. "Quartz, of course. Gold porphyry and muscovite mica."

"Any copper?" Gavin asked.

"Not that I know of.

"What have they found there?" Gavin evidently thought he was on to something.

Deedra experienced a twinge of guilt at not having told Gavin about Gregg's gem discovery.

"Hmm," Frank said. "The only thing I can think of is that in the old gold placers of California, they did find diamonds. In North San Juan they found a 7 and a quarter-carat diamond in 1867. It's a matter of record, and is the largest diamond ever recovered in California. Ever heard of diamonds found around old fossil bones?" He grinned.

Deedra giggled. "No. Nevertheless, they discovered a large gold nugget, and Von Kraus is upset about it. Since they were the only ones who knew about it, perhaps one of them is the killer."

Gavin growled, "When I came up here," he leaned back in his chair, "Von Kraus wouldn't let me near the dig, guarded it with a rifle."

"Rifle? Where is that rifle? Could it have been the one used to snipe at us?"

"I checked that out right away. It hadn't been fired in a long time."

"It isn't missing though?"

"No. It's right where he hung it after Narkette ordered him to put it away or he would arrest him for threatening people."

"Perhaps," suggested Deedra, "Von Kraus thought they would find more gold was why he was guarding the dig so closely. They said Gregg and Mary Jane weren't there when Von Kraus discovered it."

Deedra and Frank exchanged glances. They both realized that Von Kraus might have discovered Gregg's gem mine, and was certainly cold-blooded enough to have killed to protect that knowledge. He might even have hidden the nugget himself merely to cause suspicion among the others. Von Kraus was a very cold, methodical person, allowing nothing to shake his logical thinking. Deedra doubted that once Von Kraus set a goal he would deviate him from it. Had Rhonda's murder precipitated Alfred's murder? The scientists wanted to get rid of him. They detested him and if he was out of the way, it would also keep Mary Jane away from the dig.

Now only she and Brent were feared by the killer. Why? "Gavin, have you double-checked on the identity of those scientists?"

"They really are who they say they are, Deedra. Narkette fingerprinted them all right after Rhonda's murder. Nothing there. They say the fly in the ointment was Alfred Shepley."

"Hmm." Deedra didn't tell Gavin about Steven Robbins fighting Alfred and that Mark Saylen had beat him up in Boothill Alley. She glanced at Frank and he blinked.

Though the professors were pleased with Alfred's demise, she realized that it proved nothing. It did strengthen their motives. She also realized that Frank had not mentioned that he knew that Gregg had sent a copper sample in for assay. Which could just mean that the copper was from another area, possibly from Montana where Gregg had spent time earlier in the year. It could also mean that Frank and Gregg knew something they did not want Gavin to find out.

THE NEXT DAY dawned cooler, the weather showing the first signs of autumn. Deedra watched from Rhonda's window as the professors drove up the road toward the dig. Not aware that they always padlocked the door to their lab, she hurried around to Bridge Street, keeping an eye on the upper window of the hotel. She didn't want Zach to see her. It was a shock to find the newly installed padlock.

Since she still had to pretend grief over Brent, she walked with head down out the North San Juan Road.

Gregg and Frank had driven out the old stage road, but it didn't look as if they had gone up to the dig. Was Frank filling Gregg in on the fact that Brent was alive?

She circled to the northwest climbing a ridge that ran parallel with Mercury Mountain. Obviously the other mountains had been carefully searched and if Gregg had found copper she didn't think it was on either Quartz or Mica Mountain. Feather Mountain was where the professors spent their time, and would obviously have discovered anything there since they had admitted looking for the mixosaurs.

Sagebrush and mesquite grew in great thatches on the ridge, making hiking difficult. There were signs of silica; the ground was white with it. Here and there were outcroppings of quartzite. The quartz ran out near the top of the ridge where porphyry containing mica schist and gneiss, and traces of reddish cinnabar ran in direct line with Mercury Mountain. Cinnabar wasn't what she was looking for, however. A quartz outcropping surfaced at the top of the ridge. Old mine shafts filled in with erosion dotted the far slope. Evidently they hadn't been profitable.

She caught sight of rattlers gliding to shelter under heavy rocks and though she didn't hear their warning buzz, was constantly aware of the danger. Deedra made as much noise as possible knowing that if given a choice, the snakes would slither away. Despite her knowledge and the snake bite kit strapped to her belt, a shudder of revulsion shook her. Thoughts of that encounter with a rattler several months earlier caused her tremors and a tingling at the base of her skull. Colorful ring-necked lizards and the prehistoric-looking horned toads scuttled toward thick sage as she approached.

Not until she reached a clearing several yards north, almost opposite the peak of Mercury Mountain, did she breathe a sigh of relief. Rattlers would avoid that area where there was no shelter from the hot sun.

It was on that clearing that Deedra found a large green rock, opaque but not jasper. It looked as if it had fallen from the scrap jutting overhead. It was a sheer cliff going almost straight up, impossible to climb. If there was a copper deposit there it would have to be mined by skyhooks, she mused.

Glancing back toward North Ledge, Deedra saw a man vanishing into the sagebrush. He disappeared completely as if he hadn't been there. And though she watched, she didn't see him again. It wasn't Frank and it wasn't Gavin whose uniform she would have recognized even at that distance.

Aware now that she was being stalked, she cut diagonally across the east slope of the ridge, a route that would take her straight into town. She wanted to lead the stalker into a trap. He would either have to walk into the open to follow her or hide in the sage near the ridge. Being spied on was raunchy; she hated it. This whole trip had taken on the quality of a nightmare.

She pushed her fear aside and concentrated on being alert. Then she saw the man move swiftly through the sage, parallel with her trek. When she reached the base of the ridge near the North San Juan Road, Derryck Evans emerged from the thick sage shouting, "Deedra, wait up!"

She couldn't control her start of surprise. She hadn't expected him to identity himself, hadn't suspected that it was Derryck. A glance at the hotel showed Zach Johnson standing at his window and on the floor below Shelley staring out of Rhonda's window.

"Derryck! You frightened me!"

Derryck smiled in triumph.

She knew then that he had deliberately set out to scare her. He certainly was a perverse young man. She suddenly hoped that Derryck wouldn't try playing tricks on the murderer.

"I'll walk you to town. Why don't you come back to the hotel and gab with us awhile?" Derryck gestured toward the hotel. "I'm glad you moved in next door. Being alone up there at the old church was foolish."

"What were you doing up on that ridge, Derryck?"

The young man regarded her with those strange dark eyes, and then smiled complacently. "I saw you go up there. I was out on the balcony and I saw you looking for something up on the ridge." He eyed the green rock she was carrying. "Anything important?"

Deedra had the feeling that Derryck knew exactly what kind of rock she carried. "I'm a rock-hound, you know" was the only explanation she offered.

"Are you planning to leave North Ledge before winter?" Deedra inquired.

The question startled him. "No, I hadn't planned on it."

She felt Derryck's probing dark eyes on her as they walked up the street and onto the porch of the hotel. Evidently Zach and Shelley had seen them coming because they were both sitting at the plank table drinking coffee as if they had been there for some time.

The young people gathered around. Mary Jane Shepley sat on a box in the shadows next to the front window. Deedra noticed her only because she was smoking and the cigarette glowed in the shadow.

Gregg wasn't there. Valerie Penrose was sketching a tree that grew along Jackson Creek. Valerie gazed out the window at intervals, seemingly unaware of the conversation around her.

Deedra was surprised to learn that there was a clear

view of the Shepleys' house and most of Dead Man's Alley from that front window. That meant if Alfred had seen the killer that night, any of the young people could also have seen him. And had Mary Jane been out there with Alfred the night Rhonda was killed? She would remain silent because of the insurance policy, of course. If Mary Jane was suddenly involved in murder, the insurance company would be very hesitant to pay off any claim. Especially double indemnity. Again suspicions of Mary Jane surged over her. Who else had a stronger motive?

Derryck poured coffee into a granite colored cup for Deedra. The coffee was made by putting the grounds directly into the water in the largest coffee pot she had ever seen, and letting it boil. She found the coffee strong and bracing. It was heated on a Coleman camp stove, a can of white gas in the hall near the back door as the fuel.

Mark Saylen straddled an old chair, obviously enjoying the company and conversation, his attention mostly on Shelley. Deedra wondered what his ex-wife had been like, and if he had been deeply hurt by the divorce. From the looks of him now, he might even have been relieved to have that marriage ended.

She was suddenly aware that Shelley was interested in Mark, at least in their conversation, and wished she could be privy to Shelley's thoughts. Deedra might glean the killer's identity if she could. She suspected Shelley knew more of what went on in North Ledge than she let on, or had told the sheriff. Being a writer, Shelley was bound to have made observations that might have escaped the others…except perhaps Mark and Derryck. Writers have a way of observing almost by a process of osmosis. Little of what went on around them escaped their subconscious.

She had deliberately dropped the rock sample alongside Stagecoach Bridge to see if Derryck would take it later. And what would Mary Jane do if she saw the rock: examine it, leave it, or take it?

At the moment she wanted to get them talking. "Let's talk about Gregg Dancer. You know that I went to school with him. It was a shock to learn that he is suspected of killing Rhonda."

Zach threw her a shrewd glance, but said nothing. Zach was a closed-mouth type, seldom venturing opinions on anything. Deedra guessed he was probably the most intelligent of the group with the exception of Shelley Muldoon. Like most writers, Shelley had a live and let live philosophy. Zach tended to mind his own business. It would be interesting, she mused, to learn what Shelley really thought about Derryck. She wanted to read some of Shelley's writing. Deedra didn't doubt that Shelley was quite capable of following through on a murder. Shelley would know how to confuse the clues, would know how to place the physical evidence to point to Gregg. Even putting those knives in one place was a device a mystery writer might use. A talk with Shelley could prove useful.

Since no one ventured an opinion, she tried again. "You can see Mary Jane's place from here. Did any of you see Alfred on the porch the night Rhonda was killed?"

There was another silence, though Derryck winked at Deedra indicating that he had, but didn't intend to discuss it in front of everyone.

"Mary Jane, were you on the porch with Alfred that night?" Deedra was determined to get them talking.

"No, and who do you think you are, Deedra Masefield? The police? Who gave you the authority to ask us questions?" She threw Deedra a glance filled with resentment…and was it hatred?

Deedra felt as if she had just been slapped. She rubbed her wounded arm. "Isn't anyone really interested in finding the killer? Since he has made two attempts on my life, I think that gives me the right to ask questions. It's your choice whether you answer them or not."

Mark answered. "Yes, we want to find the killer, and get back to our uncomplicated lives. All this police stuff is ruining the serenity we all came up here to find." He threw a dark look toward Mary Jane who chose to ignore him.

"Was Gregg here when your group arrived?"

"No, only Frank Shundo," Derryck replied. She was slightly surprised that it was Derryck who seemed the most cooperative and wondered if there was a subtle motive behind it.

"That's not true. Gregg was living over in Crucible," Valerie retorted.

"Did you know we found Gregg's sketches over in Crucible?"

Valerie sighed. "Yes. Gregg and I went over there quite often to get away from Mary Jane."

Deedra handed her the scarf with the initials V.P.

Valerie blushed, looked at Mary Jane in defiance. "Yes, I'm in love with Gregg. Mary Jane has tried to keep us apart."

Deedra let the matter drop.

"Gregg was in the habit of visiting Crucible before that, though," Derryck murmured. "He lived over there before most of us arrived, and I suspect he had something over there he didn't want the rest of us to find."

"He's a geologist and I guess none of us asked much about his activities. It isn't really any of our business either," Mark said in a tone that indicated he wished everyone would mind their own business and let him get on with his.

Mark, with that one statement, created a barrier between them. Deedra felt depressed by it.

She glanced at Shelley, whose expression was of someone lost in contemplation. Perhaps she was thinking about her writing, trying to solve some mystery of her own.

"Valerie, has Gregg told you he was up here for any reason besides that mixosaur find?"

The girl turned her beautiful eyes on Deedra. "He said Frank Shundo called to tell him about the mixosaur find. They knew about it weeks before the expedition was sent up here. Frank had already staked out cinnabar claims for the Sierra Mining Company. He said Frank was ordered to stay up here and not let anyone in on that mercury find. They recorded all those mines before they let out word about that damn mixosaurus."

Deedra frowned. "That's odd. I got the impression that Gregg came up here just to record the geology of that mixosaur quarry."

The young people all looked at each other as if there was something they weren't telling. Gavin had said they had all been here when the scientists arrived. Had something important taken place before the dig started? Before Alfred and Mary Jane had arrived?

She decided to ask Frank about it.

NINETEEN

"DID GREGG SAY HE HAD discovered anything important up here?" Deedra asked.

Absolute silence followed her question. Their faces took on a closed look, a look that reflected Mary Jane's statement of resentment. Deedra felt hostility, and was shocked by it.

Finally, Derryck challenged, "Why do you ask?"

Deedra shrugged. "There has to be a motive for Rhonda's murder. If, as the District Attorney thinks, Gregg is guilty, then there has to be something we don't know or have overlooked."

Derryck appeared startled by her answer.

"Are you going home when the D.A. says you can, Mary Jane, or are you staying until they finish the dig?" Deedra almost held her breath waiting for her reply.

"When the District Attorney gets this case cleared up I'm going far away," Mary Jane replied in a tone tinged with bitterness.

"When did you actually arrive up here? With the scientists or afterwards?" Deedra had the conversation going now and wasn't going to stop though she already knew when the Shepleys had arrived. It was better for them to think she didn't know very much about what went on there.

"We arrived just after the others. Alfred had to wait on permission from the state to work at the dig."

"He joined the team then?"

"Just as an observer, really. He asked to help dig after a few days. It's tedious work even for those experienced in digs. They were glad of his help so we went up every day. I took notes of what they found each day for Alfred. He planned to write a book about it."

"Ah, ha," Deedra thought. Old Alfred was poaching on the professors' preserves. No wonder they didn't want him around. But they couldn't stop him. His degree entitled him to observe what they found, though he was forbidden to remove anything from the quarry itself. It didn't establish a motive for Rhonda's murder, but certainly created one for Alfred's.

A glance at Shelley showed her that the same thoughts were going through her mind. Shelley, the writer, would automatically wonder about the whom, why, what, where, when about things. Deedra silently vowed to talk to Shelley. She would improvise an excuse, and wouldn't be at all surprised if Shelley deliberately told her something important.

"Mary Jane, I was told you were overheard having an argument with Gregg near the old church the evening of Rhonda's murder?"

Mary Jane's eyes glittered. She took a drag on her cigarette before answering. "Yes, I did talk to Gregg that evening. It was just at dusk, not later. When I left him he was still up on the old stage road near the church. So I can't alibi him for the time of Rhonda's murder." She took a drag off the cigarette and watched the smoke spiral into the air.

"Nor yourself," Deedra reminded her. "What were you arguing about?"

"None of your business! You know Gregg and I were married once. And what I say to Gregg and what he says to me has nothing to do with the murders."

Deedra had to admit that it really wasn't any of her business except that it would have provided Mary Jane with an excellent alibi if she had chosen to take it.

Mary Jane watched Valerie over the glowing end of her cigarette. She was the only one in North Ledge who smoked now that Rhonda was dead. Had Valerie been the reason Mary Jane threatened Gregg? Logic told her it had something to do with Gregg's profession, though she couldn't imagine him doing anything unethical.

Watching Mary Jane she could not understand why Gregg had ever married her after having been engaged to Shelley Muldoon. Had Shelley's intelligence turned him off? Some men were annoyed by intelligent women, especially brilliant men. They associated with colleagues, but married the female myth. Surely Shelley knew that men sometimes experimented sexually, which was probably what Gregg's affair with Mary Jane had been, though she had to admit the married Gregg might have been a very different person than the one she remembered. Deedra had no clue of the traumas and conflicts of Gregg's life since leaving high school. If Shelley had done the rejecting then Gregg probably married Mary Jane on the rebound.

Deedra sighed, and tried another tactic. "Was it Steven Robbins who found Rhonda's body?" Again, she was letting them think she didn't know many of the facts about Rhonda's murder.

"Yes. We were all up and seated around the table when we heard them start the Land Rover. They called out to Gregg who usually waited for them on the far side of the bridge. When he didn't answer they drove up to his place and Steven knocked on the door. While he waited, Steven glanced into the alley. We heard him shout, 'She's been murdered!' Dr. Drake, Dr. Von Kraus, and Gregg all hurried into the alley. We all went out there, but there wasn't anything we could do. It was obvious that she had been dead for hours. Drake called the sheriff on his CB." Zach related this in a flat tone of voice as if it had happened to someone else, somewhere else.

"Did anyone touch her or search her?"

"I don't think so. I didn't see anyone do that, anyway. We could see the knife sticking in her back, and no one wanted to leave fingerprints, you know."

"Then no one had a chance to destroy any evidence?"

"No."

"Where was Frank when Rhonda's body was found?"

"Up on Mercury Mountain. He was always up and gone before anyone else," Zach replied.

"Then Frank would have had time to destroy evidence?"

"Yes, if he saw her," Zach answered thoughtfully. "Though I didn't hear his door squeak that morning." This fact seemed to puzzle Zach.

Deedra wondered if Frank had even returned to North Ledge that night, and if that was the reason he was so frightened. To relieve the mind of the real culprit, Deedra murmured, "Then Frank had plenty of time to remove the suspicious knife?"

"Yes. Either Frank didn't know that it was Gregg's knife, or he didn't see Rhonda lying there."

Shelley grinned knowingly at Deedra. What thought had just occurred to her?

She glanced at Derryck just in time to see a look of revulsion pass over his face as he stared at Mary Jane. Frank was right; Derryck loathed Mary Jane. What had she done to cause that hatred? Derryck was individualistic and definitely eccentric, but usually didn't criticize. Yet he stared at Mary Jane with a look people usually reserve for vermin.

Derryck noticed her scrutiny and was suddenly embarrassed. Deedra was amused and doubted that Derryck had been embarrassed very often.

"Did you," Deedra persisted, "know that Rhonda was Alfred Shepley's cousin?"

Mary Jane was so startled that she dropped her cigarette. "Yes, Alfred was Rhonda's cousin, though they weren't close. Their fathers were brothers."

"Rhonda was married to someone named Adams?"

"Yes," Mary Jane's voice held a venomous quality warning Deedra not to question further.

"Can anyone think of a reason why Frank would want to kill Rhonda?"

There was another silence, a shocked silence, as if this was a new thought, a new theory. No one ventured an opinion, and Deedra tried again. "Who might have had a motive for killing Rhonda?"

There were stirrings and shifting, soft indrawn breaths, but not a word. There was not even a hint of what they were thinking.

"Did anyone see anyone lingering near Dead Man's

Alley the night Alfred was killed?" She glanced out the window where a complete view of the alley could be seen through the window.

Again there was that tense silence.

"Let's not talk about the murders anymore, Deedra. We've already been questioned by the sheriff and the D.A. We're tired of it," Mark winked at her. Then she realized that she had questioned them on the one subject that caused them all uneasiness…Rhonda's murder. It was as if they thought Alfred's murder an unimportant afterthought. Though now that they knew Mary Jane owned the hotel, Alfred's murder had taken on another dimension. Now they were all on guard.

The talk shifted to art and writing, and finally Deedra got a chance to talk to Shelley and Mark. They compared experiences about writer's block, muse, plot, and character. Despite that rapport with the writers, she felt uneasy. She had seen Gavin go over Boothill Ridge earlier and knew that he had gone to check on Brent. The scientists hadn't returned from the dig.

Finally she left them, "I'm going to get a look at Rhonda's room again." She limped up the stairs with Shelley tagging along. Shelley managed to pass her a note in the midst of the silence they left behind.

The young people were not telling all they knew, and really resented her questioning them. They did not seem curious about Brent's disappearance, and seemed to take his "accident" as an unusual happening, not connected with the murders, and that one less news reporter eliminated complications in their lives.

In Rhonda's room with the door shut, she opened Shelley's note.

Deedra, I have observed these things, thought they might be important:

Gregg's knife didn't have initials on it several weeks ago when he skinned out a rabbit for Derryck.

Rhonda was in love with Gregg and hated Valerie. Rhonda met Gregg several times in front of the Wells Fargo station, and once she gestured toward the hotel. Gregg shook his head. Rhonda was very angry. It looked as if she cursed Gregg, then she ran back to the hotel.

Dr. Robbins visited Mary Jane several times when Alfred was in North San Juan getting supplies.

Dr. Von Kraus threatened Alfred and wouldn't let him inside their lab or living quarters.

Rhonda made several searches of the professors' place until they put locks on the doors.

Gregg and Frank found Von Kraus eavesdropping, and Frank threatened to beat him up if it ever happened again.

The night Rhonda was killed, Steven Robbins met Mary Jane in Dead Man's Alley, then they went inside Alfred's house.

I think the professors found more than just a mixosaur. I heard Von Kraus accuse Gregg of stealing something. Gregg said he hadn't stolen anything, especially an old fossil bone.

Rhonda was in prison years ago. I heard Alfred say, "you'd better not, you'll go back to prison again." Rhonda slapped his face. Steven was standing near the livery stable at the end of Dead Man's Alley, and saw her slap him.

Alfred Shepley had a big insurance policy, double indemnity, I think.

WHEN GAVIN'S HEADLIGHT BEAMS flashed across the windows, she hurried down the stairs without having searched Rhonda's rooms as thoroughly as she had planned. To Derryck, Mark, and Shelley, who still lingered downstairs, she said, "I've got to call my newspaper on Gavin's radio. See you all later."

Deedra was conscious of two things as she crossed the porch and stepped into the dusk of early evening. Mary Jane now thought of her as a dangerous enemy, and Derryck was afraid of her. Why, she couldn't fathom.

Gavin was standing at the hitching rail in front of his quarters.

"Everything okay, Gavin?"

"Yes. What have you been up to?"

"Talking to those young people. Did you know that now that Alfred is dead, that Mary Jane owns the hotel?"

"She what?"

"Your reaction isn't anything compared to that of those young people. Let's go inside. Shelley slipped me a note, and I want you to see it."

Gavin lit the lantern and carefully latched the door. He read the note without comment.

"Not really anything there we didn't know, but most of them didn't tell us the facts. I get the feeling talking to them that Alfred's murder was unimportant, an anti-climax, a sort of inevitable consequence."

Gavin started. "You know, Brent said almost that exact thing to me. He ventured an interesting theory about the murders. He thinks Gregg killed Rhonda, and

Mary Jane took advantage of the situation to kill Alfred and collect the insurance. He said Alfred's murder was almost inevitable."

"Oh, surely he doesn't think Gregg killed Rhonda!"

Gavin shrugged. "That's what he said, and he's had a long time to think about it."

TWENTY

"THEN WHO DOES Brent think shoved him into that old mine shaft?" Deedra asked.

Gavin scratched his head. "He thinks one of the scientists did so he wouldn't take anymore pictures of the quarry. They like to take their own pictures, want exclusive rights to them. They take pictures of each process, with the idea that it's their exclusive property."

"Were you aware that Gregg was living in Crucible until those young people arrived, that he and Frank knew about the mixosaur weeks before that team arrived?"

"Yes. I knew that, though I really don't know who alerted the university. I've heard several versions of that."

"It was Gregg who sent the first fossils to the university even though a rock-hound actually made the discovery. Alfred saw the fossils there, and had to wait until he could get permission to be present at the site. The others resented his presence, and Mary Jane was keeping notes for a book Alfred planned to write, thus earning their ire."

"Steven visited Mary Jane several times, eh?" Gavin read the note. "I doubt they had an affair going. I suspect it had something to do with Mary Jane keeping notes on the dig. Steven just wanted to know what Alfred was up to."

"Agreed, he isn't stupid, wouldn't play that game under Alfred's nose."

Gavin seemed morose after his visit to Brent, forced to realize exactly what a dangerous and intelligent killer they were trying to catch.

Deedra sighed. "We've agreed that the killer did away with Alfred because he attempted blackmail, or because Mary Jane wanted his insurance. But Rhonda's murder is the crux. If we find out why Rhonda was murdered, then the 'who' would be easy."

"Yep. But we've got to remember that murderers might have obscure motives going way back in their lives before they arrived up here."

"The M.O.'s the same, Gavin. Remember the only vital clue is that fossil bone. That has to have meaning."

"I'm not convinced of that, Deedra. Someone might have dropped it early that evening, or someone could have stumbled into Rhonda's body, dropped it, and was so shocked and scared they didn't even think to pick it up."

"The murder means are the same. Both stabbed in the back. I was stabbed. Only the attempt on Brent, and the rattler thing are different, and that was to make them look like accidents." She shuddered at the thought of the rattle-snake. "Can I see that assay report, the one Gregg sent in?"

"Narkette took it with him, but I've got a copy in my notes." Gavin handed her a report which surprisingly indicated a copper vein of no particular richness, and would probably be unprofitable to mine. Why had Gavin given her the impression that it was a rich deposit? She continued to look at it, not seeing it, pondering on its significance.

"Have you noticed that Shelley is the only one of the young people who seems at all connected to the murders?"

Gavin nodded, running a hand through his thick hair. "Yes, although I can't discount Derryck's...ah...extraordinary personality."

"I found a sample of green rock. I can use it as an excuse to get another look at the lab. I just can't help but believe that the fossil bone was a clue that Rhonda left. Rhonda was in the habit of sneaking into the lab, she might have stolen the fossil with the gold nugget, and then the killer found out. Either he just took the nugget or she was forced to give it back. If we find the nugget, we find the killer."

"That," Gavin reminded, "couldn't have been Von Kraus. He said the fossil bone was unimportant without the nugget. He wouldn't have removed it, and he's furious about its disappearance." He ran his hand through his hair again. "Careful when you go over to the lab, Deedra, those scientists mean business."

"I know. That damn rattlesnake is never far from my thoughts."

"Yeah, this is a real cold-blooded killer, has to have an unemotional, calculating personality."

"Well, Von Kraus is far from unemotional. Do you get the feeling that this is not your ordinary type killer? This is a calm, analytical type, not a tempestuous angry person."

"Yeah, and that's what worries me. I don't have the slightest notion about what he might do next," Gavin replied.

"Gavin, you know Frank would never have stabbed Rhonda in the back with Gregg's knife, though he might have done in Alfred."

"My hunch still tells me it's Derryck Evans. He's just the type to pull off something like this."

"I don't know, Gavin. Derryck seems a little afraid of me, unless I'm reading his vibes wrong. I think he knows something that is somewhat dangerous. He keeps feeding me bits of information."

A grim looks suddenly suffused Gavin's features.

Knowing the professors were back, Deedra retrieved the rock and hurried across the bridge to their lab. She wondered if they knew that she had moved into the empty building next door.

Dr. John Drake opened the door in answer to her knock. When he saw who it was he threw the door wide. "Deedra! Another visit?"

"Hi, John. I need to look at a set of *Dana's System of Mineralogy*. Do you mind?"

Deedra handed him the green rock.

"Yes, I see. This is serpentine mixed with jasper, I'd say. Where did you find it?"

"It's not a copper mineral then?"

"No," he smiled.

"I found it on that ridge west of Mercury Mountain. I looked carefully, but there's no outcropping. It's probably just float from that broken crag on Mercury Mountain."

Drake regarded her with renewed interest, though a guarded expression crept into his eyes. "And why were you looking?"

The others suddenly gathered around her.

"The sheriff wanted to know if there was any copper around here. Gregg sent a sample in for assay."

Dr. Von Kraus bristled. "That looks like copper to me. Let me see!" He snatched the rock from John Drake's hands. "Ah, not much, nothing to get excited about. I'm certain copper isn't what Gregg has discovered."

Deedra let the remark pass, but a sudden stab of fear went through her.

There was a silence while the men stared at each other. Von Kraus suddenly went off to his room.

Deedra was reminded of her errand there. "Do you mind if I look at the *Dana?*"

John Drake helped her find the information. Steven Robbins examined the green rock, and then went off to his room.

"This is a sample of porphyry serpentine, a most common and interesting rock," Drake said, "Von Kraus is mistaken, it is not copper."

She sighed. "I had visions of striking it rich." She watched Drake leaf through the book. "Did you know that now that Alfred's dead, Mary Jane owns the hotel?"

"What?" It was as if she had suddenly stuck Drake with a pin.

"Yes. I guess Rhonda and Alfred were cousins. She rented the hotel from Alfred, and then re-rented it to the young people. They knew of the place because they had been here as children. It belonged to Alfred's grandfather."

"Strange. Almost as if fate led them here to die," Drake's voice sounded strained.

Deedra shuddered. She began to wonder about Dr. Drake's philosophy.

On the wall were photographs of the men at the dig, shirtless, leaning on shovels, grinning into the camera. She studied it closely. It was evidently taken on the day they had uncovered a complete mixosaur skeleton. The pit wasn't deep. Gregg, lean and young looking, was smiling in a carefree way. Von Kraus, his chest a mat of dark hair, grinned triumphantly. Steven, the most pow-erfully built with a jagged scar across his abdomen, showed even white teeth and obvious pleasure over their discovery. John Drake was a flabby man, grinned fool-ishly at the camera as if caught with his hand in the cookie jar. Alfred wasn't in the picture, and evidently had not yet arrived.

Obviously they planned to use the photo in their pub-lished versions of the dig.

"Good clear photo." She replaced it, and then put the green rock on the long plank that served them as a work space. "Do you talk to Gregg very often? I've known him for years and he seems very uncommunicative."

Drake gave her a shrewd look. "Always the investi-gative reporter, eh Deedra?"

Deedra shook her head. "Not about Gregg. He's an old friend, as is Frank. I knew Mary Jane way back when, too. I just want to know if Gregg has really changed or if he just doesn't want to talk to me."

"Gregg is a brilliant young man. He has a success-ful future ahead of him. I guess I was as shocked as it's possible to get when Gavin said he was suspected of murdering that Adams woman." Drake paused as if care-fully gathering words. "Our talk is all scientific, nothing personal. I know Gregg was once married to Mary Jane, and I was surprised that it was Rhonda who was killed, and not Mary Jane."

"Were any of the men jealous of Gregg?"

John looked startled. "Not unless it was Alfred. Gregg isn't one to go around boasting of his accomplish-ments. Alfred obviously envied him, and he certainly wasn't the most intelligent scientist I've ever met."

"Do you think that Mary Jane could have murdered both of them?"

John Drake looked away, and took a turn about the room. "Yes, I think that's quite possible."

Though Deedra suspected Drake was hiding something, his answer did indicate that he didn't think Frank or Gregg was guilty, nor hint that his colleagues might be.

Drake ended their interview with "You'll have to excuse me now. I must wash up for supper."

Politely dismissed, she moved toward the door just as Von Kraus emerged from his room. He and Deedra exchanged nods. She noted that his door was the closest to the front door which opened without a squeak. Drake disappeared into the middle room, and that meant that Steven had the room near the back door. From that location, they couldn't be seen entering or leaving from Frontier Street.

Gavin, Frank, and Gregg were conversing in front of the old saloon.

Deedra went on to the hotel to search Rhonda's room again. Somehow she felt more secure in the hotel than she did in that empty store next to the lab. There were no dark shadows hovering about the hotel like there were from the group of trees just beyond the empty store. It was dusk, and it seemed as if the old town's ghosts were frolicking about. "I've got to get control of this imagination," she muttered as she went up the steps of the hotel.

No one challenged her right to go up to Rhonda's room where she lit a Coleman lantern. She had carefully closed the door hoping that for a few minutes at least she would not be interrupted. She pulled a chair up next to the wall. By standing on it she was just able to reach the loose board. Her hands touched paper that had been slipped into the space between the boards. She couldn't quite get a grip on it, and had to place books on the chair to stand on in order to reach it.

It was a packet that contained photographs. Nude photos of Rhonda, one of Frank making love to Rhonda, one with a man she didn't recognize. The last photo was of a group orgy with some of the participants with their faces turned away. There seemed to be three men and two women. Rhonda's body was recognizable by comparing it to the other photos. She studied the men's bodies. Only one man's face was clear enough to make out, though she didn't recognize him. She was about to replace the photos when she noticed a scar on one of the men's abdomen. It was the same scar she had seen in the photo of the men taken at the dig site. Steven Robbins. The sight shocked her.

The photo obviously hadn't been taken at North Ledge which meant that Steven had known and had sex with Rhonda before they arrived here. Steven had not admitted knowing her. The reason was obvious; still it was puzzling. If Rhonda had left the bone to implicate Steven, why hadn't he taken it when he "discovered" the body? Having sex with Rhonda might have occurred many months or years earlier and did not seem to give Steven a strong motive. Unless Rhonda was trying to blackmail him with that fact. Would it have been possible for her to ruin his professional reputation?

She started reading Rhonda's notes and skimming through her latest manuscript. It was a nauseating account of Rhonda's experiments. Unable to read further, she replaced the photos and notes.

She was uneasy about returning to the empty store. Some imp of caution warned her to remain in Rhonda's room and she lay down on the bed. It was best to wait there and return to the empty store just before dawn. The killer would hopefully not think to look for her in Rhonda's room.

The old hotel creaked and made snapping noises as it settled in for the night. She listened to soft scuttling sounds of scurrying mice. A step on the stairs screeched into the night hush causing her to sleepily wonder who prowled, alerting her to the fact that someone was up and about. Cautious footsteps passed her door and continued on. The house again settled into its nightly creaks and ghostly mutterings.

Despite her vigilance, she slipped into one of the most restful night's sleep she had since arriving in North Ledge. The thought that she had foiled the killer gave her a sense of satisfaction that filtered into her dreams.

TWENTY-ONE

IN THE WEE HOURS of the morning, Deedra heard a car engine start, then the sound of the vehicle traveling out on the North San Juan Road. She didn't waken completely, but returned to the comfort of slumber. Her awakening at daylight with early morning light filtering through the window caused a sense of confusion. It took a few minutes for her to remember where she was and why she was there. The room was cold and when she went to the window to see what vehicle was missing, an icy mist had formed on the pane. None of the vehicles were missing. Whoever had driven off in the night had evidently returned.

Gavin emerged from his office and walked across the street into Frank's place.

Deedra quickly returned to her abode, and was through with a skimpy breakfast when she heard a vehicle approaching on the North San Juan Road. A sheriff's patrol car pulled up in front of Gavin's office, two deputies got out, one carrying a heavy package.

Deedra saw Gavin beckon them to Frank's place. Was Frank about to be arrested? Not wanting to be caught spying, she watched from a back window. The minutes dragged along. At last the men emerged, and Frank himself started off toward Mercury Mountain. The sheriff and his men went across the street to Gavin's office.

Unable to restrain her curiosity, she raced around to Frontier Street, and opened Gavin's squeaky door. "Are you going to arrest Frank?"

"Nope. These are my deputies, giving me the latest on what's happening in the rest of the county." Gavin made the introductions, and the men left after politely tipping their hats to Deedra.

"No new clues or motives?" Deedra wanted to know what news the deputies had brought and couldn't ask outright.

"No. What did you learn over at the lab last night?"

"They can all sneak in and out without detection. Von Kraus knows Gregg discovered something, and admitted it in front of John Drake and me. Dr. Robbins was acquainted with Rhonda," she explained about the photos. "I guess if we find the gold nugget and the crystals that were stolen from me, we'll have our killer."

"Both Narkette and I searched everywhere after Rhonda was killed, and we didn't find any gold nugget. There are a million hiding places up here anyway."

"Since the fossil bone was found at the scene, I'm sure it has a connection to the murder. Now, Gregg wasn't at the dig when the nugget was found, and I heard them say they didn't tell him about it."

"I wonder why?" Gavin muttered.

"I suppose to keep him from sharing in the good fortune. Rhonda probably took it from Von Kraus' room. Shelley said she made regular trips to the lab when they were up at the dig."

Gavin gave that some thought. "Now, Miss Detective, what else did you learn from those young people?"

"Mary Jane might have killed Alfred for possession

of the hotel and insurance, and since she's in love with Gregg tried not to implicate him."

"You're forgetting the woman scorned thing. If Gregg ignored her advances, she might want to keep anyone else from having him, and then complicate matters by killing Alfred. That would accomplish two things for her. She would receive the inheritance and insurance, and prevent Gregg from marrying Valerie Penrose."

"You may be right," Deedra admitted. "I guess I'd better get over and see how Brent is getting along."

"You don't have to. I had Brent moved in the night. He's where the killer can't get him, and is getting medical attention. Gives us time to concentrate on the killer. I've told everyone that I have an order in for heavy equipment that we need to dig out that cave-in. I said there was some delay in getting it up here. That seemed to quell their curiosity about why nothing has been done about it."

Deedra showed her surprise, having forgotten that they would wonder why nothing was being done to retrieve Brent's body. That probably explained the deputy's visit that morning.

"Did John Drake show any reaction when he saw that rock sample?"

"Just that it looked interesting. He wasn't interested, knew immediately that it wasn't valuable. He was just polite."

Gavin stared out the window toward Jackson Creek where Mark and Zach were standing along the bank, deep in conversation.

The scientists were up at the dig and the others evidently in pursuit of their creativity.

"Have you seen Mary Jane this morning?" she asked.

"No. She has a habit of sleeping late since Alfred's death. Doesn't stir until almost noon."

Deedra was still waiting for a chance to talk to Gregg...alone. She wanted to tell him that she had discovered his gem mine and that the killer had taken the crystals from her. It didn't seem to have any connection with the murders, though from Von Kraus' remark the professors seemed to know about it. Had Von Kraus been the one who took the crystals from her jeans pocket? Or had the gem find been incidental? Did her possession of them take on new meaning for them? The killer probably carried them around with him just as she had, although like the sheriff had said, there were a million places to hide them.

She gathered up her writing materials, and returned to Rhonda's room where she wrote a feature story on the old ghost town, another about the writers/artists living in an abandoned hotel and their lifestyle there. Then she set about writing her front page story on the murders of Rhonda and Alfred, and the progress of the investigation, her rescue of Brent from the caved-in mine.

There were occasional movements in the hotel, quiet motions that were not distractive. Zach moved about in his studio overhead. Shelley was out on the balcony.

She poured through Rhonda's books, seeking to find a clue to her murder. She was thoroughly disgusted with the porno which brought a blush to her face despite the fact that there was no one there to see it. "There might be something to book burning, after all," she muttered.

From the window she noted the emptiness of the street. A noise overhead reminded her of Zach, who seemed to lack a motive for either murder, Zach who tried to remain out of attention's way.

She hadn't yet told Gavin about Frank's confession, his connection with Rhonda. Was it possible that Rhonda had alliances with all or at least, most of the men at North Ledge? She definitely had sex with Steven Robbins, had it continued here? Carefully she went over ever word, every incident, Brent's accident, and the stalker in the night. It hadn't been Frank, of that she was certain. She wouldn't have been able to hide from him on Mercury Mountain.

Methodically she fit every person into the role of killer. The killer had been afraid of coyotes, and Frank and Gregg were not afraid of them. She concluded that only Kurt Von Kraus, Steven Robbins, and Mary Jane had enough motive and opportunity. They fit the profile, all with cold analytical personalities, capable of acting and with complete self-control. A cold strategist. Uneasily she admitted that part of the puzzle was yet to be ferreted out.

Frank was still up on the mountain, the scientists at the dig. No one ventured onto the dusty street. Still, she remained at the window, pondering, speculating. Who had taken the map? After a time, a plan occurred to her, a strategy that she hoped would reveal the killer's identity. She had to make certain that everyone knew where she went, had to arouse the killer's curiosity.

She rushed down the stairs, giving Shelley a "see you later" wave. Out in front of her new abode, she checked the emergency supplies in her 4-wheel rig, made certain she had everything she needed to protect herself… except her gun. She had given it to Brent.

A surreptitious glance showed Mark standing on the balcony with Shelley, Mary Jane seated on her front porch. They watched her in silence, obviously curious.

Since she was hampered by the sprained ankle, she had to rely on the rig to take her as close to Gregg's find as possible. But first she was going to stop at the dig and let the men know she was on the mountain. The killer would want to know why since she obviously couldn't hike any distance. And she was certain that Gavin would watch through binoculars…hoping he would watch.

She drove out the old stage road raising a cloud of dust, across the creek, and waved as she roared past the men at the dig, then up the draw between Feather Mountain and Mica Mountain. Then she zigzagged across Mica Mountain to within shouting distance of Gregg's mine. From that point she couldn't be seen from North Ledge or from the dig site.

Nevertheless, she circled around instead of going directly to the gem claim. Occasionally she picked up a rock, examined it, and then threw it away. All with that paranoid feeling that accompanies surveillance by others.

At last she kneeled near the boulders that camouflaged the vug of gems. Her heart thumped with excitement. Unearthing the vug she dislodged a large tourmaline crystal which in turn uncovered a valuable aquamarine. She drew in a breath of awe. The crystals glittered in the sunlight. She put them in her jeans pocket, and then recovered the vug, wiped out the traces of disturbance.

She continued to circle the area, continued looking for something, occasionally picking up a rock, then discarding it. If Frank watched he would be puzzled, if

Gregg watched he would be anxious. If Gavin watched he would merely think she was indulging in her rock-hound hobby.

Finally she piled several rocks on top of each other, then stepped off thirty paces down the mountain where she placed rocks on a boulder. A glance toward North Ledge showed no movement. She could only hope that Gavin had seen her action.

The sun's position overhead told her it was noon; time to visit the fellows at the dig. She tried to drive across to Quartz Mountain in a slanting direction, but was forced to go back and retrace her tracks, then cross over to the dig.

The men were eating lunch in the shape of a gnarled tree which looked as if it had been planted in the Jurassic age.

Deedra waved a greeting and limped to the dig. Her reporter's alertness registered the fossils, the depth of the quarry, how wide it was, found no signs that it had been camouflaged. She felt the eyes of the men speculating on just how dangerous she was to their endeavor.

"Cup of coffee, Deedra?" John Drake offered.

"Yes, thanks. I've been up on Mica Mountain. This mountain air sure works up an appetite."

Drake laughed, and told her of an incident when certain colleagues at the university hadn't known what an apatite crystal was, and the hilarious results. They talked about the quarry, what they expected to find, when they reckoned their work would be completed.

Gregg was strangely quiet as if he found it difficult to talk to Deedra.

A strong north wind sprang up causing a sudden

change in the weather. Dark clouds rolled into view like tumbleweeds propelled by an unseen hand.

"There's going to be a storm." Von Kraus apologized as they scurried to gather up their tools.

Standing at the edge of the quarry, she brushed back her flying hair, then took out a bandanna which threw two crystals on the ground at John Drake's feet.

"What's this, Deedra?" John's hand shook as he picked them up.

"The result of a rock-hunting trip," Deedra replied, replacing the gems in her pocket. Her reply was vague enough to give the impression that she had found them at some other time and place. Only Gregg and the killer would know differently. She was aware of Von Kraus' stare, Steven's renewed interest, Gregg's pale face. She knew they were all wondering why she had let them see the crystals, suspected that she had done it deliberately. At least the killer would suspect that.

As she climbed into her rig she was aware of their stares, aware of the killer's dangerous vibes which seemed to reach out to her with real anger, furious that she had set him up with a false map.

She waved goodbye and roared down the mountain, smiling and shivering at the same time. The first drops of rain hit the windshield with a splatter that rained mud down the glass. By the time she reached the old stage road, the rig was slithering in mud.

Gavin's rig was gone.

She went up to Rhonda's room to change into dry clothing. There was something about that old store that caused shivers, and she avoided spending time there. In Rhonda's room she drew another map, one with the stone markers on it, and placed it in her notebook. This time she had placed the boulders and rocks on the North Ledge side of the mountain where the place could be observed through binoculars. As an afterthought, she drew a sketch like Gregg's from memory, and even noted the formula for the beryl mineral, (aquamarine), Be Al Si O.

THE STORM LASHED ABOUT, rain splattering against the old buildings, and running in rivulets across Frontier Street creating thick mud. Puddles collected at low places in Dead Man's Alley. The men arrived from the dig, sodden, and glum. She saw Gregg race to his place.

Frank opened his door, looked toward Gavin's, then realizing that he wasn't there, shut the door vanishing from view.

Just as rapidly as the storm had arrived, it passed over, leaving only a monotonous drizzle, muddy puddles, and Jackson Creek overflowing its banks.

Two days passed and the trick of letting the professors see the crystals hadn't seemed to work. No one made any attempt to steal them or to look at her notebook, though she had left it in her abode next to the lab. She began to wonder if her suspicion that Steven Robbins was the murderer was wrong. Perhaps Gavin was right, and it was really Derryck Evans.

Three more days passed without any new developments. Clete Bailey via Gavin's police radio urged her to return to the city. She begged for more time and he reluctantly gave her three more days. She had to solve the murder in that time or go back to the *Daily Spokesman* without that frontpage story.

THAT DAY Deedra discovered Brent in Frank's house. The discovery was quite accidental. Deedra had been on her way from her new quarters to the old hotel, and had cut between her place and Frank's to reach Frontier Street when she heard someone sneeze in Frank's house. She had just seen Frank climbing about on the mountain.

Thinking she was about to catch Derryck or Mary Jane snooping, she hurried around the old store, and quickly opened the door.

"Don't move!" A gun was pointed at her head. Deedra saw a face loom out of the semi-darkness. "Brent! How did you get here?"

Brent grinned and gestured for silence. After laying the gun on the table wrote something on the page of his notebook.

"No one is to know I am here. Gavin had a neurosurgeon from the city dress up like a sheriff's deputy and examine me. I'm okay. Gavin and Frank moved me here during the night."

Deedra wrote down the killer's identity, and how she was trying to trap him. After Brent read the note, agreed that she was right. Deedra lit a match and burned the note. She looked up to find Brent staring at her with a look of admiration. She knew he was thinking of the scoop they were going to get.

Suddenly he pulled her into his arms, and whispered that he exercised at night when everyone was sleeping. That he had seen the killer outside several times. Once he had actually seen Steven go up onto the porch of the old hotel. Brent had thrown a rock into the road behind him, scaring him away.

Deedra whispered that she hadn't told Gavin about her plan.

Brent insisted that she tell him as soon as possible.

To prove that his accident hadn't incapacitated him, Brent made love to her right there in Frank's shack. She hoped that no one was outside listening.

A storm prevented the men from going to the dig the next day. Their presence in North Ledge changed Deedra's plans about going up on the mountain. Instead she limped to her new residence where she scribbled notes and ideas for future stories, then started reading one of Shelley's mystery novels. Exciting though it was, she found her mind wondering.

Gregg had gone to the hotel and was probably talking to Valerie. She had intended to talk to Gregg, let him know she had found his gem mine, but he didn't give her a chance. Why was he avoiding her? Was her presence in North Ledge embarrassing to him?

Later that afternoon the sun replaced the storm clouds. The old ghost town steamed from the damp ground and mud puddles. By evening the puddles had dried up, though the air still felt damp. Deedra headed for the hotel with the intention of talking to Shelley. She didn't hear a sound as she passed Frank's place, and though tempted to stop, she did not.

She suspected that Shelley had left several important facts off the list she had given her. Outside Shelley's room she heard the sound of typing, and waited until there was a pause in the steady clicking before she knocked.

"Who's there?" was the cautious reply.

"Deedra. Am I interfering with your creative muse?"

"No," Shelley laughed, and threw the door wide. Tendrils of her dark blonde hair curled about her face, and there was a smudge of typewriter ink on her chin. It was obvious that she had been working for several hours. Character sketches were taped to the wall above her typewriter.

They began discussing writing. Deedra learned that Shelley had a mystery novel being considered for an award. Shelley was child-like in her enthusiasm and half-surprised that she could be considered for an award. Deedra related her own efforts at novel writing, and some of the cases she had investigated. Shelley was intrigued with her adventures and asked if she wished she had taken Abram's offer of marriage.

"Are you planning to write a novel about it, Deedra?"

"I have, but probably won't ever get around to it. I seem to have one investigative assignment after another, and never settle long enough for prolonged creativity. Besides, I'm still looking for a guy to marry. If I'm to have a family, I have to get started soon."

"I thought there was a guy in your life. What's his name? Deke Thomas?"

"Well," Deedra drawled, "Deke just isn't the marrying kind, and I've ruled him out, Brent Larsen is more my type."

"You had a thing for that Brent Larsen, didn't you?"

"Yeah." Deedra felt it wise not to get started on the subject of Brent. She might give away the fact that he was still alive, and within a few leagues of them, already regretting the use of the present tense in referring to Brent. Shelley was bound to pick up on that.

"That's another plot I plan to use someday, but I see

you are thinking that if I didn't care, you might make use of those ideas. Right?"

Shelley flushed. "Yes. You know writers; we're always looking for material. I could use you as the protagonist, you know, and get most of the story from the newspaper."

Deedra grinned. "Just make sure you check with me before publishing anything. I am sort of possessive about my writing, too."

Shelley laughed. "You know that as long as it's in the newspapers, it's fair game."

"Yeah," Deedra sighed.

Shelley sobered. "Have you discovered who killed Rhonda and Alfred?"

Deedra gave her a long look. "Yes. I'm trying to trap the killer. It's difficult up here at North Ledge without modern conveniences, though."

"Someone I know?" Shelley laughed, then sighed. "I hope you have solved it, Deedra. And I hope it isn't anyone living here at the hotel. I'd hate to think that I'd been sharing meals with a killer." She glanced about the room. "It isn't Gregg, is it?"

Deedra shook her head. She knew that was the closest Shelley was ever going to admit that she was still in love with Gregg. It wasn't, however, her only reason for asking. She wanted to find out if Deedra suspected her, and was doomed to disappointment if she thought Deedra was going to take her into her confidence.

"I can't tell you without proof, Shelley. Sorry." She watched the young woman mask her disappointment. "You haven't thought of anything else that has escaped the sheriff's attention?"

"One thing. A man came to see Steven Robbins about three weeks ago, that is three weeks before Rhonda was killed. I overheard Gregg tell Valerie that Steven was very upset after the man left."

"Hmm. Gregg seems to be avoiding me. Do you have any idea why?"

"Really? I imagine he's wary of your being a news reporter. Maybe he's afraid of a story, 'How I killed Rhonda Adams,' by Gregg Dancer as told to Deedra Masefield."

Shelley grinned.

Deedra wasn't amused, but it was an insight that hadn't occurred to her. "Have you any theory about the killer?"

Shelley gave her a straight look. "I hope it's Mary Jane, but I'm afraid it isn't." Then she laughed. "I can use that in a book someday though."

Deedra spent the evening in Gavin's office discussing the murders. She didn't tell the sheriff her theory, someone might be eavesdropping, and she wanted to give the killer time to search her place.

When she arrived at her "residence" she was instantly aware that the killer had been there. The fine spider web she had strung across the door was broken, her notebook had been moved, though nothing was missing. A shiver of danger shook her. She placed a heavy rock in front of the door and shined the lantern into all the murky corners to reassure herself that no snake lurked there.

The night passed quickly, Deedra only dozing at intervals though knowing that the killer couldn't search the mountain at night. It was her own safety she was anxious about. He had made two attempts, the third might succeed. She listened to the sound of a coyote's yelp, the twittering of birds, the soft noises that couldn't be identified, but were part of night in the mountains.

At last sleep claimed her, and she didn't hear the soft opening of her door, how it hit against the rock. The killer decided against entering, knowing he would cause too much noise, noise that would rouse Deedra and she would scream. He gritted his teeth in frustration. Deedra had already fooled him with that map. He wanted to make her pay.

The District Attorney arrived early and disappeared into Frank's place with the sheriff. Frank was already up on the mountain. Mary Jane had observed their activities from the hotel balcony.

Deedra saw Zach walk past his window, and vanish into his sanctum, and was reminded that Zach was like a shadow, present but seldom talking, allowing himself to meld into the background, doing nothing to call undue attention to himself. He was undoubtedly a very talented artist, probably brilliant of mind, had resented Rhonda, she was certain that he was relieved over Rhonda's demise. She had no inkling of what he thought of the others living at the hotel. He was friendly enough, just reserved.

By mid-afternoon the weather had turned hot, and everyone sought the shade along Jackson Creek. Deedra sat on the bank where she could watch Mica Mountain. She hoped the trap would spring while the D.A. was still in town. It didn't.

The day dragged on as if it was pulling something heavy uphill. Deedra pretended to read, but watched both the mountain and Frontier Street, and stayed away from her place.

At 4:30 she went to Gavin's office and requested the use of the police radio. Gavin didn't try to listen to her conversation with Clete Bailey.

"Clete, you had better record what I have to say so you can scoop the other newspapers. I've found out who the killer is," she hissed. Quietly she told him what amounted to a frontpage story, then added the information that Brent was in Frank's abode, and how the sheriff had smuggled a physician up to examine him.

"Brent's all right then?"

"Yes. I've told him who killed Rhonda and Alfred just in case the killer gets me." Deedra didn't elaborate. "Gavin doesn't know that I know that Brent is here. He tried to give me the impression that Brent had been taken back to the city." Deedra paused. "Can you find out if Gregg had that claim recorded?"

"I can already answer that. He recorded it last spring before the scientists got there. Evidently he's waiting for them to clear out before doing anything about it. And being suspected of murder would make him reluctant to do anything."

Deedra contemplated that news.

"Anything else?" Clete asked.

She told him about Dr. Von Kraus finding a gold nugget in a fossil bone, and how upset he was that it was missing.

"Deedra, that's so fantastic I hesitate to print it."

"Well, don't until we find it. Then we can run it with those features along with the news of the trial. That ought to sell papers."

Clete laughed. His excitement about the scoop, a coup really, was evident in his tone. It didn't happen often enough to dull the thrill of beating other newspapers to the news.

"Don't let on to anyone else that you know who the killer is," Deedra cautioned.

"What's the matter with you? You know I wouldn't do a thing like that!"

Deedra laughed. "Prepare to give me those bylines, Clete."

AT 5:00 DEEDRA saw movement on Mica Mountain. At first she thought it was only a deer, then after a long interval saw the killer's rig in the draw just east of Gregg's find. It was Steven Robbins causing her a sense of sorrow. She had to admit she had wanted to be wrong. With the fake map she hurried to tell the sheriff that the killer had taken the bait.

"If that guy moves those rocks off that boulder and tries to move the boulder itself we can be certain he's the killer," Gavin growled. "How do we trap him, though? Just because he moves those rocks doesn't make him guilty of murder in the eyes of a jury."

"First we have to get Mary Jane to admit that Alfred saw the killer go into Dead Man's Alley just before Rhonda was killed. Then I'll tell you how."

They watched through the binoculars as the man on the slope stepped off thirty paces, removed the rocks and pushed the boulder aside. His gesture of anger caused Deedra to shudder. Now the killer knew that it was a trap. Now he would try to stop her before she could tell anyone about it. She didn't try to explain why it was important that Mary Jane admit that Alfred had told her he had seen the killer.

The sheriff went out and in a few minutes returned with Mary Jane who wasn't at all pleased to be questioned again.

"Mary Jane, we've discovered an interesting clue and since your husband was murdered, I think it's wise for you to level with us," Gavin glanced at Deedra. "Did Alfred see someone go into the alley just ahead of Rhonda that night?"

It was obvious that Mary Jane hadn't expected the question. Her pupils enlarged until her eyes looked black. "Who told you that?" She didn't deny it or admit it.

"Just that we know it. I'm sure you don't want to get on the witness stand and tell any lies. You're the major suspect, you know."

Mary Jane flinched as if Gavin had slapped her. She glanced at Deedra, frightened and perhaps for the first time in her life, unsure of herself.

Deedra felt sudden sympathy for the woman.

Mary Jane took a deep breath, her voice tight, squeaky. "Yes. We were on the front porch. I went inside to mix us a couple of drinks. Alfred said he saw Steven Robbins go into the alley, and then Rhonda followed him. He laughed, and said Old Rhonda had made another conquest. We didn't realize right away that it was Steven who killed her since Rhonda liked to rendezvous with the men at night." She paused and took a long drag on her cigarette. "I didn't want Steven after me! If I pretended that I didn't know anything I was safe. Steven did question me, but I pretended that I had been inside that night and didn't see anything. I said I didn't think Alfred had either because he didn't tell me he had." Mary Jane expected the sheriff to see the logic in her reasoning, and indeed, she was still alive because she had pretended not to know anything

"It was Frank's knife that killed Alfred, but whose knife stabbed Rhonda? It wasn't Gregg's."

There was a flicker of fear in Mary Jane's eyes as she answered. "It was mine. An old one I kept from the time when Gregg and I were married. Steven must have taken it that afternoon when he visited while Alfred was in North San Juan getting supplies."

"Steven visited you often?" Gavin asked.

She glanced away, took a deep breath. "Yes. I planned to divorce Alfred after we returned to the city. Steven and I were to marry then, but I'm not going to get involved in these murders for him." Her voice has a shrill quality, a note that told of her fear.

"Did Steven know Alfred left a large insurance policy?" Gavin couldn't keep the sneer from his tone of voice.

"Yes. I think Steven has financial problems."

Deedra suddenly realized that Mary Jane had only been leading Steven on, had never intended to marry him, was just afraid of him. She wanted nothing to interfere with her claims on the insurance.

"Did you look for your knife after Rhonda's murder?"

"Yes. It was gone. There was a knife like it there, but it wasn't mine."

"Why didn't you tell the D.A. or me right away?"

"Alfred told me not to. He said it was too dangerous and reminded me that I'd been married to Gregg, and that put me in a very tenable position. He said that it suited him for everyone to think that it was Gregg's knife." She paused and took another drag on her cigarette. "I think he wanted something from Steven. Now I'm sure of it." Her voice dripped bitterness.

When Mary Jane left, Gavin told Deedra to go up on the mountain where Frank was, "The killer can't get you there. I'm not going over to the lab and give anyone's attorney an opportunity to say I didn't have a search warrant. We'll just have to wait until Steven Robbins gets back."

Deedra did as she was told and found Frank just as he walked out of a deep mine shaft. They sat in the cool entry out of the hot sun, and she told him what they had discovered, what Mary Jane had told them

"What if it isn't Steven? Just because he went into the alley ahead of Rhonda doesn't prove he's the killer?"

"Mary Jane said he followed Rhonda into the alley, and Alfred made some snide remark about Rhonda having made another conquest. If we find the gold nugget and the crystals he stole from me, we'll have him. His greed has trapped him, and he's in financial trouble according to Mary Jane."

STEVEN RETURNED with the others, and no one had approached Mica Mountain.

She and Frank went directly to the sheriff's office when they reached town.

"Deedra, you're to stay here tonight. I'm not ready for you to act as bait for a trap. I'm going to watch through that knothole in the wall there. I'll be able to see anyone that tries to get into that old store. I'm not going to try to stop them tonight. It's just a test to make certain Robbins is the murderer. So far the evidence against him would be laughed out of court. A smart lawyer could get him off. Brent didn't see his assailant, so can't swear that it was Robbins. Just because he took a fake map doesn't mean he killed anyone. We've got to prove it with evidence that can't be dismissed by a jury."

It was difficult for her to sleep that night.

The sheriff sat by the wall watching through the knothole. There was moonlight so that the buildings stood out in dark silhouette. By midnight there were only nocturnal noises, the night birds were quiet, the coyotes silent.

Deedra was on the edge of sleep when she heard Gavin say, "Ah."

Steven had left his quarters, stood for a time looking about, then stealthily entered Deedra's temporary abode in the old store. He was inside only a few moments, then reappeared and rapidly returned to the lab.

"He knows you aren't in there now, he won't try looking anymore tonight," Gavin whispered, then settled on his cot and was soon snoring.

Before daylight Deedra was back in her residence, and emerged just as the men got ready to leave for the dig. She saw Steven start when he saw her. She waved and went over to Gavin's office.

They watched as the Land Rover disappeared in a veil of dust. The rain never seemed to conquer the dust there.

"You do believe it's Steven now?"

"Yep," Gavin replied with a heavy sigh.

"What do we do?" Deedra knew what she planned, but wasn't yet ready to tell the sheriff.

"We'll just wait and let things happen. The opportunity will arrive if we just let the stew bubble and brew. The killer's uneasiness is catalyst enough."

Deedra was impressed by the sheriff's knowledge of human nature. Gavin was an enigma; not at all like another sheriff she knew whose personality was so definite without hint of mystery. Gavin had a kind of mysterious mien about him, as if he knew something important all the time that he was keeping secret. She didn't tell him that she knew Brent was in Frank's place, and wasn't sure why. Even though she knew that he didn't tell her all he knew, sometimes she felt as if she was dueling with him. Did he resent her ability? Did he dislike it that she understood more about what the scientists were doing than he did?

The day passed slowly, no one ventured up Mica Mountain.

A very frightened Mary Jane spent the day on her front porch. The sheriff spent some time talking to her, but didn't divulge what he had learned, to Deedra's frustration. She was forced to sit along the bank of Jackson Creek and read a book.

The men returned at mid-afternoon. It had turned hot, and they complained of headaches.

After they'd had time to settle in, Gavin and Deedra walked over to the lab, and as they crossed the bridge, Gavin cautioned. "Now, Deedra, if it isn't the right time, just let it go."

The men seemed glad to see them. After they discussed the mixosaur for several minutes, Gavin asked, "Is it true, Dr. Von Kraus, that you found a gold nugget embedded in one of the fossil bones?"

There was a tense silence while Von Kraus looked

from Drake to Robbins, then back to the sheriff. "Yes, it's true. Have you found it?"

"Is it missing?" Gavin asked.

"Yes. I've looked everywhere for it. I left it in my bedroom; it was in the fossil bone then." Von Kraus glared at Drake and Robbins.

"Is that the only fossil you found with gold or anything else in it?"

At Deedra's question Von Kraus relaxed a bit. "Yes. The fossil evidently moved upward through the area where the gold is. It was not 'in situ,' you understand. Not surprising really. This is old gold country."

While Gavin interrogated Von Kraus about the nugget, and why the fossil bone had been left beside Rhonda's body, Deedra wandered about the lab. She felt Von Kraus' ferret gaze, and John Drake's probing watchfulness. They were probably still wondering where she had found those crystals.

She heard Gavin ask, "How big was the nugget?"

"About the size of a walnut, a perfect nugget. Worth perhaps half a million dollars embedded in that fossil bone. Only now it's just worth the going rate of gold sold by the ounce." Von Kraus was clearly upset.

She had not expected the nugget to be of such value, hadn't realized that it was as large as a walnut, unusual in any event. Only the murders had prevented Von Kraus from calling more attention to its disappearance.

She saw Gavin straighten in his chair when learning of the nugget's value, and laughed to herself. There was nothing like a money motive to attract a lawman's interest.

Taking books down from the shelves and casually leafing through them, she then selected a volume of

Dana's System of Mineralogy, and took it back to a chair next to Gavin. She idly leafed through it while alert to every nuance in Gavin's interrogation.

"Was it missing before Rhonda's murder? I mean a day or two before, or didn't you miss it until after it was found beside her body?"

"I missed it that day when we returned from the dig," Von Kraus replied.

"Do you think Rhonda took it?" Gavin asked.

"I suppose she did since the fossil was found beside her," he retorted.

"We didn't find the nugget on her though, nor was it in her room."

"Of course not. The killer took it!" Von Kraus acted as if Gavin couldn't figure that out.

"We've searched all the houses, and we didn't find it. I want your cooperation. I want you all to allow me to search your clothing. The ones you are wearing."

Deedra held her breath.

Von Kraus sighed. "All right. I'm sure you need a warrant to do that, but I have no objection. If you think I stole it from myself, you're sadly mistaken." Von Kraus turned his pockets inside out.

Steven Robbins quickly grabbed a hunting knife that had been lying on the counter, put a hammerlock around Deedra's neck, and backed toward the door.

"Don't anyone try to stop me or Deedra gets it!" he snarled.

Gavin halted in the action of reaching for his gun, dropped his arm to his side.

Deedra squirmed, desperately tried to get away, but Steven had an iron grip, and backed her to the front door.

"Remember, Deedra gets her throat slit if any of you try to follow me!"

She knew he would not let her live. She had trapped him, and for that he would make her pay. Her heart beat in slow painful throbs.

There was sudden vague movement when Robbins opened the door.

Suddenly his grip around her throat loosened, and he fell to the floor unconscious.

Brent Larsen moved into the room and stood astride Steven Robbins brandishing a wooden mallet. He grinned in his crooked way from under the head bandage.

"I couldn't let him kill you, Deedra. Who else could I get to winch me out of dark tunnels?" His eyes caressed her.

"Brent!" She threw herself into his arms while Gavin galvanized into official action.

After the handcuffs were on Robbins, Gavin searched his pockets and found a flattened gold nugget. It belonged to Von Kraus.

He held it up for everyone to see. "This it?"

"Yes. I suppose he flattened it for easier carrying. Gold is very malleable, you know."

Gavin just raised his eyebrows, and continued searching Steven's pockets. He found the crystals that had been stolen from Deedra.

"I can't believe it was Steven!" John Drake stared with obvious incredulity at the unconscious man.

"He wanted you to think Gregg took it," Deedra reminded.

Von Kraus asked, "Why did he use Gregg's knife on Rhonda?"

The sheriff gestured for Deedra to answer.

"He didn't. He stole a knife from Mary Jane. It was a knife that Gregg had owned when he was married to her. Gregg had forgotten it, of course. It was she who had scratched the initials on it after their divorce. Steven stole Frank's knife to use on Alfred."

"So he tried to make it look like Frank murdered Alfred. Why did he kill Rhonda?"

"Rhonda had damaging photos of Steven taken during an orgy. She threatened to use them to stop his promotion to head paleontologist at the university. It's such a prestigious position she could ruin his reputation easily enough. The gold and gems would ease him out of his financial trouble."

"Alfred was killed because he saw Steven that night?" Drake asked.

"Yeah, and Alfred made impossible demands," Gavin replied. "Not money, just an advancement to head up a unit in the science department."

Brent was grinning and taking pictures when it suddenly dawned on both Drake and Von Kraus that Brent was still alive.

Brent's explanation of what happened eased any doubt the men had that Steven was the culprit. Brent's accident had occurred on a day when Steven had supposedly driven to North San Juan. He had returned to the dig with rust on his shirt. Evidently he'd had trouble getting that old ore cart moving and it had ruined his shirt. They had even teased him about poking around old mining equipment.

Steven regained consciousness, and when he saw Brent standing over him, fainted again.

"Brent," Deedra said when all the questions had been answered, "let's go over to my place. I haven't thanked you properly for saving my life, saving me from that creep!"

She gave Steven Robbins a look that should have caused him deep pain.